"Do you always visit

"No," said Thea. ""

"Well, I hope it isn't your last, seems to like you."

"She said this was her fourth time in the hospital," Thea said. "I can't imagine what that must be like."

"It's hell," Kip said. "Maybe a little bit worse than hell."

"You must all be looking forward to when she gets home," Thea said.

"Gina isn't coming home," Kip replied.

"You mean you're moving?" Thea asked. "Gina said your apartment was small."

Kip stared at Thea. "I mean Gina's going to die here," he said. "She's never going to get well enough to come back home."

Oh, God, Thea thought. Nicky, what have you gotten me into?

"You didn't know?" Kip said. "Nobody told you?"

"No," Thea said . . .

Titles in *The Sebastian Sisters* series by Susan Beth Pfeffer, published by Bantam Books:

EVVIE AT SIXTEEN
THEA AT SIXTEEN

Forthcoming titles:

CLAIRE AT SIXTEEN
SYBIL AT SIXTEEN
MEG AT SIXTEEN

THE SEBASTIAN SISTERS
THEA AT SIXTEEN

Susan Beth Pfeffer

BANTAM BOOKS
NEW YORK · TORONTO · LONDON · SYDNEY · AUCKLAND

THE SEBASTIAN SISTERS: THEA AT SIXTEEN

A BANTAM BOOK 0 553 40146 7

First published in USA by Bantam Books, a division of Bantam Doubleday Dell Publishing Group, Inc.

First publication in Great Britain

PRINTING HISTORY
Bantam edition published 1991

Copyright © 1988 by Susan Beth Pfeffer
All rights reserved.

Conditions of sale:
1. This book is sold subject to the condition that
it shall not, by way of trade *or otherwise*,
be lent, re-sold, hired out or otherwise
circulated without the publisher's prior consent in
any form of binding or cover other than that in
which it is published *and without a similar condition
including this condition being imposed on the
subsequent purchaser.*
2. This book is sold subject to the Standard Conditions
of Sale of Net Books and may not be re-sold in the U.K.
below the net price fixed by the publishers for the book.

Bantam Books are published by Transworld Publishers Ltd.,
61–63 Uxbridge Road, Ealing, London W5 5SA,
in Australia by Transworld Publishers (Australia) Pty. Ltd.,
15–23 Helles Avenue, Moorebank, NSW 2170, and in New
Zealand by Transworld Publishers (N.Z.) Ltd., Cnr. Moselle
and Waipareira Avenues, Henderson, Auckland.

Made and printed in Great Britain by
BPCC Hazell Books
Aylesbury, Bucks, England
Member of BPCC Ltd.

This time—for Allison

THEA
AT
SIXTEEN

CHAPTER ONE

"**W**hat a dump."

"I wish you'd stop saying that," Thea Sebastian said to her sister Claire. "You say that about every place we move into."

"They're all dumps," Claire replied.

"At least we own this dump," Sybil Sebastian said. "Have we ever owned our dump before?"

Thea and her two younger sisters turned to their oldest sister, Evvie, aged eighteen and family expert, for the answer. "I think we may have owned one years ago," she said. "Right before you were born, Claire. But we've rented ever since then."

"And now we own," Thea declared. "And Megs will get to really work on the house, turn it into a mansion. You wait and see, Claire."

"This house will never be a mansion," Claire replied. "Maybe less of a dump, but no mansion."

"Think how much better it is than that awful place we had in Harrison," Evvie said. "A couple of years ago, when we first moved there."

"The house was awful, but I liked Harrison," Sybil said. "I don't see why we had to leave there."

"We left because Nicky thought he could do even better here in Briarton," Thea said. "And the way Nicky's been going, he's bound to be right."

"He's on a lucky streak," Claire said. "It'll never last."

Thea stared at her sisters. Evvie was two years older than she was; Claire, two years younger; and Sybil, four years younger. Except for Claire, Thea loved them all, almost as much as she loved her parents, Nicky and Megs. Except for Claire, they were the perfect family: close, caring, and full of fun. She wished she could believe Claire was a foundling, some unrelated baby Nicky and Megs had taken in as a misguided act of charity. But while she, Evvie, and Sybil all had Megs's blond coloring and blue eyes, Claire, with her black hair and blazing green eyes, was every inch Nicky's daughter. Not that Claire liked Nicky. Not that Thea liked her.

"I know this house feels like a comedown," Evvie said. "That last place in Harrison was pretty spectacular."

"We each had our own room," Sybil said. "I never had my own room before."

"But it was a rental," Evvie continued. "And you know how much it means to Megs to have a real home, a place she can work on. So we share again."

"That's easy enough for you to say," Claire replied. "You're going off to college in a week. Then Thea gets the room all to herself. Meanwhile Sybil and I have to share for the rest of our lives. It's so unfair being younger."

"Sometimes I think everything's unfair," Sybil said, and Thea turned to pay attention to her. Sybil didn't waste much time complaining.

"We've already explained it to you. Opportunities were better here," Thea said. "Don't you want Nicky to be real rich again?"

"If that would only happen," Claire said. "Were we ever really rich, Evvie? Tell us about the richest we ever were."

Evvie laughed. She curled up on the floor next to her bed, and rested her feet on an unpacked box. "I guess we never were as rich as Aunt Grace or Clark," she said. "They own their mansions. But once, long ago, Nicky did have a major boom and for a year or so we were wonderfully rich. Then the boom busted. The mansion we lived in vanished, and the servants we had vanished, and the only things we had left were each other and our memories."

"I don't even have the memories," Claire complained. "All I ever remember is us being poor and pretending not to be."

"That's better than being poor and acting like you're poor," Thea declared. "Besides, we aren't poor now. So stop whining, Claire, and hand me that box."

"Sometimes I feel like all I ever do is unpack," Sybil said. "This is our third home in two years. My entire childhood has been spent in a suitcase."

"Think how I feel," Evvie said. "I don't know whether I'm packing or unpacking. When we left Harrison, I know I put everything in a deliberate order so I'd remember what I was leaving here, and what I was taking to

Harvard. But now it's all a jumble, and I have to start all over again."

"Harvard," Thea said. "You're actually going there."

"In a week," Evvie said.

"That's another thing that isn't fair," Claire said. "We've already started school, and you have another whole week."

"I wish I was there already," Evvie replied. "It's driving me crazy that I have a week left to go."

"Because you want to be in school, or because you miss Sam?" Thea asked.

"Both," Evvie said.

"You really are lucky," Thea declared. "You go off two summers ago, to spend time with Aunt Grace in Eastgate, while we're stuck in that terrible house in Harrison, not knowing a soul, and you fall in love, and you stay in love, too. Just like Megs when she met Nicky the summer she was sixteen."

"Except Sam is reliable," Claire said. "Unlike Nicky."

"Do you really think you and Sam are going to get married?" Sybil asked.

Evvie nodded. "But not until I'm through with college," she said. "That's why we're both going to Harvard. So we can be together while we wait."

"I hope I fall in love," Thea declared. "I've been sixteen for three months already, and I haven't met anybody to fall in love with except the guy who drove the moving van."

"Love is overrated," Claire replied. "I don't want to waste my time being in love. I want to be rich instead."

"You can be both," Thea said. "Ever hough money doesn't really matter."

"I don't want to be piddling rich," Claire said. "I want to be so rich I can eat diamonds."

"I just want to be rich enough so that I can live in one place forever," Sybil said. "When I'm grown up, I never want to pack or unpack again."

"I won't care what my life is like," Thea declared. "Just as long as I'm as much in love with my husband as Megs is with Nicky. The way you and Sam are, Evvie."

"That'll happen," Evvie promised. "Just give yourself some time, Thea."

"I'm tired of waiting," Thea grumbled, and then she laughed. "I sound like Claire," she said. "Yuck."

"Yuck to you, too," Claire said. "Come on, Sybil. We have our own stuff to take care of."

"Okay," Sybil said. "See you later." She followed her older sister into their bedroom.

"Are you sure you labeled some of the boxes Harvard?" Thea asked Evvie when they were alone. "I remember you said you were going to."

"I was going to do lots of things I never got around to," Evvie replied. "I'm afraid I'm going to be leaving you with an awful mess."

"That's okay," Thea said. "It'll make me feel better having your things around. Maybe I'll miss you less that way. We've moved so often, you've always been my one best friend. And now we've moved again, only this time you won't be here for me."

"Oh, Thea," Evvie said, and she got up and hugged Thea. "I'm going to miss you so much."

"As much as you miss Sam when you're not together?" Thea asked.

"Differently," Evvie said.

"Tell me about love," Thea said. "I know I'm always saying I'm in love, but I want to know what it's really like. I am sixteen now. I'm the age girls in this family fall truly and permanently in love. So tell me what to expect."

"Look, Thea, I never expected to fall in love when I was sixteen," Evvie said. She opened up a box, stared into it, sighed, and closed it again. "Sam was an accident that summer. He was there, and I was there, and that was it."

"But suppose you hadn't met him that summer," Thea said. "Suppose you met him next week at Harvard. Would you fall in love with him then?"

Evvie nodded. "I'd fall in love with Sam if we were both seventy-five years old and married forever to other people," she replied. "I know that's how Nicky and Megs feel, too, kind of preordained. But I don't think all love works that way. Maybe just the spectacular kind."

"That's the kind I want, then," Thea said. "And I want it now."

"Take my word for it, it's easier if you wait," Evvie declared. "Sam's grandparents aren't real thrilled that we're still in love. And frankly, Nicky and Megs haven't been crazy about the idea, either."

"Because Sam's Jewish?" Thea asked.

"Because he's different," Evvie replied. "He isn't what they would have picked for me, and I'm certainly not what the Greenes would have picked for Sam. Not that everyone hasn't been very friendly and tolerant. But it would have been easier if we'd met later, when we were older. Maybe seventy-five. By then the Greenes wouldn't care."

"I know Nicky and Megs will like whoever I fall in love with," Thea said. "This box is definitely yours, and it's definitely stuff you want to take with you, Evvie. Check it out."

"Good," Evvie said. "This box is yours. It's all your poetry books."

Thea walked over and moved her box to her side of the room. "Last year, when we had money again, I kept buying poetry," she declared. "I didn't read nearly as much of it as I meant to. Maybe this year I'll read it all. Sometimes I think I'd like to be a poet."

"Great," Evvie said. "There's a lot of money in that."

"Now you sound like Claire," Thea said. "I want to be so rich I can eat poetry."

The girls laughed. "I wish you weren't going," Thea said. "I wish you could stay here forever, and things could be the way they always were. I didn't even like us having separate bedrooms last year. I like sharing everything with you, Evvie."

"Life doesn't always work that way, Thea," Evvie said.

Thea grinned. "I may be a romantic, but even I know that," she said. "Everything changes. Mansions come and go. It's only love that lasts forever."

"Love and zits," Evvie said. "I've had one right under my chin for ages now."

"Let me look," Thea said, and she was engrossed in Evvie's skin problems when Megs knocked on their door.

"Supper's ready," Meg said. "I see you've gotten a lot done here."

"We talked," Evvie said. "I can never talk and unpack at the same time."

"We've been in this house for almost two weeks," Meg said as she escorted her daughters downstairs. Thea could hear Sybil and Claire already in the kitchen. "And the house looks like we arrived here yesterday."

"You're being impatient, Megs," Evvie said. "You

own this house. You can take as long as you want to get it looking just right."

"It's nice to think that way, but it really isn't true," Meg replied. "Nicky wants us to start entertaining as soon as possible. And I can't have anyone over with the place looking like this."

"I'll do more tomorrow, I promise, Megs," Thea said. She did feel guilty over how little she'd done. Claire and Sybil already had their bedroom set up. Sybil, she suspected, had done all the work, while Claire bullied her around, but whatever the system, it had proved more efficient than her and Evvie's trick of falling into conversation and leaving the boxes right where they were.

"It's my fault, too," Evvie said. "I really thought I'd packed better when we moved, but now, each time I open a box, I find half the stuff is going with me, and the other half is staying, and the thought of having to repack everything depresses me so much I don't get anything done."

"I know," Meg replied. "Nicky says we can afford a piano, and half of me is so excited that I want to go out and buy it right now, and the other half of me says, wait, get the wood stripped and the walls painted before moving a piano in. So I don't do anything. I just sit around the living room and daydream about how lovely it will be to have a piano to play again."

Thea looked at her mother. Megs had grown up orphaned, in the house of her aunt Grace. Aunt Grace wasn't the warmest, most loving person around, but she had provided Megs with everything a proper girl from proper society should have. And that included a piano. The plan had been that Megs would fall in love with and marry someone equally appropriate from Boston society, probably Clark Bradford, who'd been in love with her since the day Megs stopped wearing diapers. But instead, on her sixteenth birthday, Megs had met Nicky Sebastian, also an orphan, but one without money or social position. None of that had mattered. They'd fallen in love, and in spite of Aunt Grace, had eventually married, and continued to love each other while raising four daughters, and dealing with the ups and downs of Nicky's fortunes. Now the fortunes were up, and Megs could have her piano again.

"I'll help tomorrow," Thea said. "I don't have much homework. I'll get it all done in the morning, and then you can order me around in the afternoon. That way you can get the piano sooner."

"Thank you," Meg said. "I appreciate all your help. Sybil's been especially helpful. I think she should be a restorer when she grows up, someone who cleans old paintings or rebuilds cathedrals."

"What do you think I should be?" Thea asked. They were almost at the kitchen, and she wasn't sure she wanted Claire to hear Megs's answer, but it was one of those opportunities that might never come up again. Did Megs think she should be a poet? Or the perfect homemaker, the way Megs was? Thea was never sure what she wanted her future to hold, and she liked the idea of having Megs tell her what to do.

"I really don't know," Megs replied, which surprised Thea, who believed Megs knew everything. "Sometimes I think you should be a teacher, or have lots of children. You have such a capacity for loving and caring. But other times I want you to be an explorer, to chart unknown worlds. I guess I like the image of you in a pith helmet."

"An explorer?" Thea asked.

"I'm never going to be an explorer," Sybil called from the kitchen. "Explorers have to unpack all the time."

"They have servants and guides who do it for them," Claire said. "It would be fun to be an explorer if you got to keep everything you found. Diamonds and emeralds."

"What do I get to be?" Nick asked, coming in from his office. "Assuming I bother to grow up?"

"You get to be my husband," Meg said, giving him a kiss. "A full-time job."

"I can't think of a better one," Nick said, and he returned Megs's kiss. Thea was accustomed to the constant signs of love between her parents. She was taken aback at other people's homes, where the parents didn't hug and kiss and lose themselves in each other's eyes.

"The person we should be asking about careers is Evvie," Meg said. "Have you thought about your major?"

"I've thought about it endlessly," Evvie replied. She walked over to the stove and started carrying the chicken curry to the table. "I haven't decided yet. Sam's majoring in journalism, but he's always known he wants to be a reporter. Sam wants to tell people the truth about things, and he figures the best way to do that is by reporting."

"There's no money in reporting," Claire said.

"Nobody's asking you to be a reporter," Thea said. She brought the homemade chutney to the table, as well as a dish of slivered almonds. "Who'd believe anything you wrote, anyway?"

"What did you want to be, when you were a kid, Megs?" Sybil asked. "When you grew up?"

"I never gave it much thought," Meg replied. "We were all programmed then, to be debutantes and brides and young mothers. I guess I expected to wear white gloves and attend cotillions until the day I died."

"What about you, Nicky?" Thea asked. She sat down at the table, and poured herself some juice. "What did you want to be when you were a kid?"

"I wanted to be out of there," Nick said, glancing away for a moment. "I wanted to be all the things I wasn't."

"You got what you wanted, then," Evvie said.

"I got all that and more," Nick replied. "I never could have dreamed, when I was a boy, of a girl like Daisy." Daisy was the private name he used for Megs. "And I certainly never could have pictured myself as a family man, proudly sitting in my kitchen, surrounded by four exquisite daughters. I knew I wanted money, when I was a kid, but it never occurred to me I could have love as well."

"What did you dream about?" Thea asked. Her father rarely talked about his childhood, and they all knew better than to ask. But this seemed to be one of those rare evenings when he might open up and tell them things they would never otherwise learn.

Nicky laughed. "I had an image of a great marble palace," he said. "I guess I must have seen it in a movie somewhere. And I was going to live there, the richest man in the world. If you'd told me then that I'd enjoy eating in the kitchen, I would have laughed in your face. We always ate in the kitchen, because we didn't have a dining room. I thought, if I'm ever rich enough to have a dining room, I'll never eat in a kitchen again. And here I am, in a house that I own, that definitely has a dining room, merrily eating in the kitchen."

"We don't have any dining room furniture," Claire pointed out. "It's either the floor there, or the table here. Please pass the raisins."

Thea did, cursing Claire silently for breaking the mood. "When we get dining room furniture, we can eat there all the time," she said. "What else did you dream about, Nicky, when you were a boy?"

"Nothing important," he said, and Thea could see his mood had changed. "Besides, dreams don't count unless you do something with them."

"That's what I intend to do this year," Thea said. "I want to turn my dreams into reality."

Claire snorted. Even Evvie looked amused.

"Well, I do," Thea said. "I'm just not sure which dreams."

"I have an idea, if you're interested," Nick said. "I was talking to Ed Chambers this morning. He owns some radio stations in the area. Nice fellow."

Thea didn't bother to wonder how Nicky could have met someone like that in the week and a half they'd been living in Briarton. It was Nicky's way to meet important people. They always liked Nicky, and soon investment possibilities were being discussed, and Nicky was putting big deals together, and everybody made profits. That was what Nicky did for a living, that was the way he operated.

"What did Mr. Chambers say?" Meg asked.

"He's head of the fund-raising committee for the hospital," Nick replied. "I mentioned that I'd done a bit of fund-raising back in Harrison, and naturally we talked about different techniques."

"Oh, Nicky," Meg said. "I can't have a fund-raising party here. Not when we don't have furniture."

"I'm not asking you to," Nick replied. "Ed's wife heads the volunteers at the hospital. Apparently, they can never get enough people for all the work that has to be done."

"They're going to have to get by without me for a while, too," Meg declared. "This house is my first priority, Nicky. Once we're settled in, then I'll put in a few hours a week at the hospital."

"But in the meantime, why can't Thea do some work there?" Nick asked. "They're delighted when teenagers come in to help. And Ed and his wife are two people in this town it pays to make happy."

"What would I have to do?" Thea asked.

"Nothing you can't handle," Nick assured her. "Probably just bringing newspapers and magazines around. Plumping pillows. Smiling and making patients feel better."

Thea looked at her father. Plumping pillows hadn't been her idea of how to make her dreams come true, but clearly Nicky felt it would help him with his. "If I hate it, can I quit?" she asked. It never hurt to know the ground rules.

"With my blessing," Nick replied.

"All right, then," Thea said. "I guess I'm a volunteer."

CHAPTER TWO

"Oh, good," Nick said to Thea the following Thursday. "I see you're home from school."

"I just got in," she replied. "Where is everyone?"

"Daisy's out shopping," Nick said. "Evvie's upstairs pretending to pack. And Claire and Sybil both have after-school activities. It'll give us a chance to talk."

"About what?" Thea asked. She put her books down on the living room sofa and wondered what was going on.

"I ran into Ed Chambers this morning," Nick replied. "He said his wife was still waiting to hear from you."

"Who's Ed Chambers?" Thea asked. "Oh. His wife. The hospital, right?"

"Right," Nick said. "You promised on Saturday you'd see her about doing volunteer work."

"Nicky, I forgot all about it," Thea declared. "I'm sorry. I'm still trying to get the swing of the new school, all those new people to meet and everything, and I flat-out forgot."

"I wouldn't have brought it up in the first place if I hadn't thought it was important," Nick said. "I try never to ask things of my daughters unless there's a real reason to. And in this case, there's a reason. We want to make a good impression in Briarton, Thea. Your cooperation is vital in helping our family out, especially now that Evvie is leaving for college."

Thea nodded. She could count on one hand the number of times Nicky had scolded her. It occurred to her that she had always been good because she hated the consequences of being bad. "I wish you'd reminded me," she said. "It isn't that I don't want to do the volunteer work."

"You're sixteen years old," Nick said. "I had assumed I could trust you to remember. I see I was wrong. Would you like me to dial the number for you?"

"What number?" Evvie asked, walking down the stairs. Thea was never so happy to see her sister in her life. "Hi, Thea. I thought I heard your voice."

"Evvie, Thea and I are having a private discussion," Nick said. "Concerning family cooperation."

"My favorite topic," Evvie replied. "Wait while I get an apple."

And there was something about Evvie that made Nicky and Thea wait until she came back from the kitchen, apple in hand. "All right," Evvie said. "You can resume your private discussion."

Nicky shook his head. "Evvie, you're incorrigible," he declared.

"I know," she replied, taking a bite out of the apple.

"It was my fault," Thea said. "I was supposed to call the hospital about being a volunteer and I forgot."

"I don't blame you," Evvie said. "Do you really want to be a volunteer, Thea?"

"No," Thea replied. With Evvie there, she decided on being honest. "It doesn't sound like any fun. I'd rather help Megs with the house."

"You can do both," Nick said. "Nobody's asking you to work at the hospital seven days a week."

"Thea doesn't want to work there any days a week," Evvie declared. "I don't see why she has to."

"For starters, because I told Ed Chambers she would," Nick said. "And how can I expect men like Ed Chambers to trust me if I prove untrustworthy about such small things."

"You shouldn't volunteer people without asking them first, then," Evvie said, and punctuated her remark with another bite of apple. Watching her chew reminded Thea of how hungry she was. Still, she knew this was no moment to break away and get something to eat.

"This really isn't any of your concern, Evvie," Nick said. "Thea agreed to call and I expect her to live up to her word. A couple of hours a day a couple of days a week isn't going to kill her. And not only will it help them at the hospital, but it will help us as well. We're a unit, this family, and we should always be willing to help each other out."

"Thea's no traitor," Evvie said. "She forgot to do something because she didn't want to do it in the first place. It's no big deal."

"It's a big deal to me," Nick replied. "And it should be a big deal to Thea."

"It is," Thea said. "I mean, I'll do it. I'll call Mrs. Chambers right now and make an appointment, and I'll do the volunteer work. I am sorry, Nicky. It was dumb of me to forget."

"Fine," Nick said. "The name and number are right by the phone in the kitchen."

"It is not fine," Evvie said. "Thea, if you don't want to do it, don't. You have no right to bully her this way, Nicky."

"I am not bullying her," Nick said, and Thea could see how angry he was. Thea hated the idea of Nicky being angry, and she especially hated the idea that she was responsible.

"Of course you are, Nicky," Evvie said. "You should hear yourself. Family responsibilities. Family unity. You sound as though, if Thea doesn't come through, your entire empire will collapse."

"My empire, as you call it, is sending you to Harvard in a few days," Nick declared. "My empire has sheltered you and clothed you and given you advantages you take for granted. I've never seen you turn down any of the good things family unity and responsibility and empire have offered you."

"No?" Evvie said. "Well, maybe I should have. If the price for going to college is letting you have your own way about everything, then maybe it's too high a price."

"And how have I had my way as far as you're concerned?" Nick asked. "What dreadful things have I forced you into?"

"Spending that summer at Aunt Grace's for one," Evvie said. "I was just like you, Thea. Better to agree than to upset poor Nicky."

"That summer turned out really badly for you, too,"

Nick said. "A summer at Eastgate where you fell in love. You must regret every minute you spent there."

"There were a few that weren't so great," Evvie said. "But the point is you never really gave me the chance to say no. Just the way you're refusing to listen to Thea now."

"There's a tone in your voice I haven't liked for a while now," Nick said. "You came back with it after that summer, Evvie. I've always assumed it has something to do with Sam, some attitude of his you've picked up."

"It has nothing to do with Sam," Evvie said. "I went away from home—you sent me away—and while I was gone, I had a chance to see your empire from a different perspective. That's all."

"There's more to it than that," Nick said. "There's a hostility, a lack of respect."

"If you mean that I won't be bulldozed anymore, you're right," Evvie declared. "No matter how charming you can be."

"Will the two of you stop it!" Thea said. "Evvie, thank you for defending me, but it isn't necessary. He's right. I told him I'd do the volunteer work and I will. Nicky, Evvie's going to college in three days. You don't want to be angry at her, and Evvie, you don't want to be angry at him, either. There's no reason for anybody to be angry at anybody else. I said I was going to call and I'll do it right now. I hate it when people are mad at each other in this family. I don't even like it when I'm mad at Claire, and she drives me crazy. Please. We're different from other families because we do love each other, and it's stupid when we fight, and I won't have you fighting because of me. So just stop it."

"Fine," Evvie said. "I never meant to upset you, Thea."

"You're right, Thea," Nick said. "I must have sounded petty to you, and to Evvie. Will you just make that call?"

"Right now," Thea said, and she ran to the kitchen phone, and dialed the number. She asked for Mrs. Chambers and was put right through. It was hard to remember what she had to say, when she was still shaky from the scene in the living room, but she managed to introduce herself and apologize for having taken so long to call.

"Nonsense," Mrs. Chambers said. "I've been impatient only because I was so excited that you plan to volunteer. Your father speaks of you so glowingly, I know you must be a remarkable young girl, dedicated to helping others less fortunate than yourself."

"I don't know how remarkable I am," Thea said. "Or dedicated. But I would like to try."

"Do you have any preferences as to where you'd like to work?" Mrs. Chambers asked. "We can use a good volunteer anywhere, so if there's one place in particular, I'm sure we can place you there."

Thea tried to think what place in a hospital she'd dislike least. The gift shop occurred to her, but she wasn't sure the hospital had one, and besides, it sounded like a cowardly and materialistic refuge. "I don't know," she said. "I like children. And I do have a couple of younger sisters."

"Then we'll put you in pediatrics," Mrs. Chambers said. "Oh, I have a wonderful idea, if you think you're up to it."

"What's that?" Thea asked. Pediatrics sounded okay to her. Bunches of basically healthy kids getting over asthma attacks and broken legs. She could play with them, read out loud to them. Megs had mentioned teaching as a possible career for her. Volunteer work in a pediatrics ward might be a good start.

"This could be very difficult," Mrs. Chambers said. "So you don't have to give me an answer right away. I'm sure your instinctive response will be to say yes, because the kind of girl who volunteers to work in a hospital and who loves children will be thinking of them first and not of herself. So even if you agree right now, I won't hold you to it. You can think about it over the weekend, and come in on Monday to talk to me and see if you still want to do it."

"Do what?" Thea asked. Mrs. Chambers could give Nicky a few lessons in bulldozing.

"The hospital has a special program for its children with cancer," Mrs. Chambers said. "We're very fortunate to be one of the best cancer-care facilities in the area, and we have children from a hundred-mile radius who stay in the hospital while undergoing treatment for their illnesses. What we like to have is a one-on-one relationship between a volunteer and one of our childhood cancer patients. Naturally there are never enough volunteers, and the work can be emotionally very draining. Have you had any experience with cancer, Thea?"

"Not personally," Thea said. "I've never been sick with anything much in my life."

Mrs. Chambers laughed. She sounded like Glinda the Good. "I meant, have you known anyone with cancer?" she said. "Sometimes I get so excited, the words come out all wrong."

"Oh," Thea said. "Well, no one in my family." She thought about it for a moment, and realized one of the true advantages of having attended seven different schools was that she'd run into at least one of everything. There had been Betsy in third grade. She'd worn a stocking cap because her hair had fallen out. And Rob in sixth grade.

And last year, what's-her-name, Michelle, who was still undergoing treatments when the school year had ended. "Yes," she said. "I have known a few kids with cancer in different schools I've gone to."

"So you would know what to expect," Mrs. Chambers said. "It can be very lonely for these children, even those who live right here in Briarton. Oh! We have the sweetest little girl here right now, being treated for leukemia. We all love her. Her mother works, so she can only spend limited amounts of time with her daughter, and it would make all of us feel so much better if this little girl had a volunteer friend. We call them Friendly Visitors. You'd almost be a big sister to her. You'd visit with her a couple of times a week, talk about the sorts of things girls love to talk about, not about illness or family problems, but happier things. Do you think you might be interested in helping us that way, Thea? Would you like to be a Friendly Visitor?"

Thea knew she didn't dare say no. Anyone as noble and dedicated as she was, had to say yes, even if she then thought about it over the weekend and changed her mind. Not that she was sure she would change her mind. Being a Friendly Visitor didn't sound any worse than fluffing up some old person's pillow or making change for some doctor in a hurry. "It sounds really interesting," she said. "Can I come in on Monday and learn all the details?"

"Oh, Thea, you are as nice as I thought you'd be," Mrs. Chambers declared. "What time shall I expect you on Monday?"

"I'll come straight from school," Thea said. "Three-fifteen, three-thirty? Is that all right?"

"I'm putting you right down in my calendar," Mrs. Chambers said. "I can't wait to meet you, Thea. And

21

spend the weekend thinking about being a Friendly Visitor. The pluses are enormous, the gratification is beyond your wildest fantasies. But it can be hard as well, depressing when the treatment isn't going well. So I won't hold you to your yes."

"Thank you," Thea said. "I'll see you on Monday, then."

"Thank you," Mrs. Chambers said. "Have a nice weekend."

Thea hung up the phone and wondered what she'd gotten herself into. Mrs. Chambers was about to nominate her for sainthood when all she'd done was what Nicky had told her to do. She wished the idea had been hers to begin with. It felt uncomfortable getting credit for something that had been imposed on her.

Nicky wasn't even in the living room as she walked out, so she went back to the kitchen, poured herself a glass of milk, and cut a slice of the zucchini bread Megs had baked the day before, and carried them up to her bedroom. Evvie was lying on her bed, ignoring the dozens of half-packed boxes that surrounded them both.

"I'm sorry," Thea said as she sat down on her bed, balancing the milk and bread carefully.

"Sorry about what?" Evvie asked. "Boy that looks good. I'm going to miss Megs's cooking when I go away."

"Sorry that I made you and Nicky fight," Thea replied. "Would you like some?"

"Thea, if I want any bread, I'm perfectly capable of getting it for myself," Evvie said. "You don't have to offer me sacrifices."

"I didn't mean to," Thea said. "It's just that it's a big piece and I thought you might like some. That's all."

"Oh, Thea," Evvie said with a sigh. "I'm the one who's sorry. You have nothing to apologize for."

22

"I know you think you have to protect me sometimes," Thea said. "I guess I like it that you do. Sometimes I envy Sybil because she has all of us to protect her. You don't have anybody. I mean, I'll protect you, but it's not the same as having a big sister."

"I don't need protecting," Evvie said. "And you don't, either, Thea. I stepped in because Nicky drives me crazy sometimes, the way he orders all of us around. He even tries it with Claire, and Claire never does what you order her to do, so he's crazy to approach her that way. But that's how Nicky is sometimes. Crazy."

"I wish you wouldn't talk that way about him," Thea said. She took a large bite of bread, and washed it down with milk. "Nicky isn't at all crazy. And you have to admit he loves us."

"Oh, yeah," Evvie said. "I admit that, all right."

"Then why do you sound that way?" Thea asked. "Like you know Nicky loves us but you don't really believe it."

"Because things aren't as easy as you want them to be," Evvie replied. "Thea, I love you, but the only person I've ever heard you say anything bad about is Claire, and Claire drives you so crazy it's amazing you haven't tried to murder her."

"I don't understand," Thea said. "What's wrong with not saying bad things?"

"Nothing," Evvie said. "But weren't you angry at Nicky just now? He did force you into something you didn't want to do."

"I know it seems that way," Thea replied. "But he's right about the family and how we all have to help out. And he's right about you, too. You never used to talk to him the way you did today. But ever since you met Sam, you've had a different attitude about Nicky. Claire and Sybil have noticed it, too, and frankly, I don't think it sets that great an example for them. Especially Claire. What is it about Sam that made you change the way you feel about Nicky?"

"It has nothing to do with Sam," Evvie said. "At least not the way you think it does. But I'm not going into gory details now."

"I don't know what I think," Thea said, gulping down the rest of the bread and milk. "And I don't know what you mean. Except I liked it better when you didn't pick fights with Nicky. And that's just what you did today, Evvie. You picked a fight with him for no reason whatsoever."

"I thought there was a reason," Evvie said. "He was bossing you around and I didn't like it."

"So you bossed me around instead," Thea declared. "You acted like I couldn't be trusted to handle myself with him."

"Well, you can't," Evvie replied. "You always give in, Thea. You always do exactly what Nicky tells you to do. Sometimes I think it would be better if you were more like Claire."

"I never want to be like her," Thea said, surprised at how angry Evvie was making her. "The only person Claire loves is herself. I love everybody in this family."

"That's not true about Claire, and anyway, it's beside the point," Evvie said. "I worry sometimes that you don't give yourself a chance to be happy, especially when you think that what you want might upset Nicky. Megs, too, for that matter. Or even me, offering me that damn slice of bread when it was obvious how hungry you were. Thea, you're never going to get what you want out of life if you keep giving things up to make everybody else happy. That's all. I want you to be happy. I want you to eat your own stupid slice of bread. I want you to stand up to Nicky if he volunteers you for something you don't want to do, and then gets angry at you for not doing what he volunteered you for in the first place."

"Fine," Thea said. "I promise you I'll do everything to make me happy, even if it breaks everybody else's heart. When you come home from college, you'll find a second Claire in this house. We'll see how much you like it then."

"One Claire is enough," Evvie said. "As is one happy Thea."

But I am happy, Thea protested silently. How can I not be happy when I come from a family I love so much? Only there was no point in telling Evvie that. She was leaving the family. Or maybe she had already left it, left it the day she fell in love with Sam.

No matter what changes happen in my life, Thea promised herself, I'll keep on loving Nicky and Megs, and Evvie, and Sybil, and even Claire. Her heart was big enough for all of them, and she was going to do whatever she could to see to it that they were always happy. That would make her happy, so they were all even.

CHAPTER THREE

"**C**ome in, Thea. What a beautiful girl you are."

Thea entered Mrs. Chambers's office and was amused to see that Mrs. Chambers actually looked like Glinda the Good. She smiled and sat down on a chair next to Mrs. Chambers's desk.

"You must look like your mother," Mrs. Chambers declared. "Your father's coloring is so dark."

"I do," Thea replied. "My sister Claire is the only one who really looks like my father."

"Four daughters," Mrs. Chambers said. "I always wanted to have a sister. I have two brothers, both older than me. I never lacked for protection, but there was no one to share secrets with."

Thea thought about Evvie, who'd been gone for just over twenty-four hours and who she already fiercely missed.

"My oldest sister, Evvie, started college yesterday," Thea said. "We shared everything. She's at Harvard."

"Harvard," Mrs. Chambers said. "Well, isn't that impressive. Your family must be bright as well as beautiful."

"Evvie certainly is," Thea replied. "I'm going to miss her so much. That's one reason why the Friendly Visitor program sounded so interesting to me. It's a chance for me to do something so I won't think of Evvie quite so much."

"Then you are still interested," Mrs. Chambers said. "Oh, I am delighted. And I'm sure you'll love Gina, the little girl I told you about last week. We all just love doing things for her. Would you like to meet her?"

Thea nodded. "What should I know about her first?" she asked.

"Oh, not that much," Mrs. Chambers said. "She has leukemia, which used to be fatal in just about every case, but lately there have been some real breakthroughs in treatment, and there's a sixty-percent survival rate in its childhood form nowadays. This isn't Gina's first stay at the hospital, so she's an old pro, but there's nothing tough or hard about her. Her family is from Briarton, so her mother and her brother visit daily."

"Why is she getting a Friendly Visitor, then?" Thea asked. "I'd think you'd use them more for kids who live further away."

"That's how we usually place them," Mrs. Chambers said. "But Gina is a special child, and the days here in the hospital are very long. I'll tell you what. Why don't I introduce you, and if the chemistry is right, then you can be her Friendly Visitor. If one or the other of you has reservations, which I just can't see happening, then we'll find another child for you to visit with. All right?"

"Fine," Thea said, getting up. Mrs. Chambers smiled at her, but didn't offer her any ruby slippers to click. Instead they walked through several hospital corridors, leaving Thea lost and confused. She'd need a Friendly Visitor herself to guide her through the hospital maze.

"It seems confusing now," Mrs. Chambers said, "but after a couple of times here, you'll know your way around. All hospitals are like that, confusing at first, and then you feel at home."

Thea wasn't sure she wanted to feel at home in a hospital. She hadn't had much experience with them except on TV shows.

"This is the wing we want," Mrs. Chambers said. "And Gina's ward is right through this door." She opened it, and Thea was relieved to see it didn't look much worse than a dormitory. Not that she'd had much experience with dorms, either.

There were six beds in the room, and four of them were occupied. The room was large and sunlit, and there were toys casually scattered in one corner. Each bed had its own table, and the pictures on the walls were of teddy bears and rainbows, the sorts of things grown-ups often figured kids would like. Two of the kids were sleeping, one was crying, and one was reading. Thea was relieved when they walked over to the bed of the girl who was reading.

"Gina Dozier, I'd like you to meet Thea Sebastian," Mrs. Chambers said. "Thea, this is Gina, whom I've told you so much about."

"Only good things," Thea assured Gina, checking her out as casually as she could manage. She was surprised to see how old Gina was, eleven or twelve was her guess. Somehow she'd pictured a much younger girl, five or six, cuddling with a doll. Instead Gina was reading *TV Dreamstars* magazine. Thea had read it herself at that age.

"Gina, you know about our Friendly Visitor program," Mrs. Chambers said. "Bucky and Marie both have Friendly Visitors who come to see them. Well, Thea would like to be your Friendly Visitor. What do you think about that?"

Gina stared at Thea, who blushed.

"Only if you like me," Thea said. "If you don't like me then I don't have to be your Friendly Visitor."

Gina smiled then, and Thea started to understand why Mrs. Chambers thought Gina was so special. It was a beautiful smile. Gina was too thin to be pretty, but her smile lit up the room. Thea smiled right back at her.

"Why don't I leave you girls alone for a bit," Mrs. Chambers said. "You'll have a chance to get to know each other. Thea, after you and Gina are through, come back to my office, and we can discuss matters. Ask anyone for directions. Gina, dear, I'll see you later."

Thea watched as Mrs. Chambers deserted her. She didn't know what to do or say, until Gina pointed out a chair by her bed. Thea sat down in it and smiled some more.

"Do you get paid for being a Friendly Visitor?" Gina asked.

Thea shook her head. "It's volunteer work," she replied. "Why?"

"I was just wondering," Gina said. "I've seen them visit Bucky and Marie, and I always wondered if they got paid to. Bucky's getting radiation treatment now. That's Marie in that bed there, crying. She cries all the time."

"I guess having a Friendly Visitor isn't the answer to all your problems, then," Thea said. "Unless she's crying because of her Friendly Visitor."

Gina smiled. "She's crying because her parents are getting a divorce and she feels like she's responsible. Because she's sick. If she hadn't gotten sick, she figures they wouldn't be getting divorced. Are your parents divorced?"

"No," Thea said. "They love each other a lot."

"My parents are divorced," Gina declared. "Sometimes I think it's because of me."

"I'm sure it isn't," Thea said. "People get divorced all the time whether their kids are sick or not. Lots of times they get divorced and they don't even have kids. I wouldn't worry about it, if I were you."

"I don't," Gina said. "Not like Marie. Besides, my parents have been divorced for ages. I haven't even seen my father in four years. Kip says he could even be dead. Dani says she hopes he is."

"Who are Kip and Dani?" Thea asked.

"My brother and sister," Gina replied. "They're both older than me. I'm twelve. How old are you?"

"Sixteen," Thea said. "And I have a sister who's just your age. Sybil. And another sister, Claire, who's fourteen, and another sister, Evvie, who's eighteen. No brothers, though."

"Kip is eighteen," Gina said. "Dani is fifteen. That's short for Danielle. Is Thea short for something?"

"Just Thea," Thea replied. "Is Gina short for something?"

"Just Gina," Gina said. "I'm the youngest. I'm in sixth grade. What grade is Sybil in?"

"Seventh," Thea said. "She just started."

"I've missed lots of school," Gina said. "This is my fourth time in the hospital. Have you ever been in a hospital?"

Thea shook her head.

"You're lucky," Gina said. "They take your blood all the time, and they give you medicines that make you throw up and your hair falls out and after a while your friends don't come and visit anymore. They think leukemia is catching, or maybe they just don't like watching me puke. This is my own hair, though. Bucky's bald and Marie's hair is falling out. Those two kids sleeping are new here. I don't really know them. I like Bucky. He's ten, but he's smart for his age. Marie's okay when she isn't crying."

"I'd cry, too, if my hair was falling out and my parents were getting a divorce," Thea said. "Don't you ever cry?"

"Sure, sometimes," Gina said. "Not as much as I used to, though. The first time all my hair fell out I thought it was kind of funny. I was real little then. The second time, I cried. By the second time my dad was gone."

"Did you miss him?" Thea asked.

"I missed my hair more," Gina replied. "What's Sybil like?"

"She's funny," Thea said. "She saves all her money, and she's always figuring out ways to get some more. She loves to read, we all do, but she never buys any books. She takes them out of the library instead, because they're free. And she does wonderful things with her hands. She can fix things and strip down old furniture and paint really delicate things. She had a doll-repair shop last year. Kids would bring in their broken dolls and she would fix them, even paint their fingernails and toenails. She does very well in school, too."

"Does she have lots of friends?" Gina asked.

"She has enough," Thea replied. "We move around a lot. It's hard having friends when you move around."

"We move, too," Gina said. "The place we're living in now is really bad, it's so small. Dani and Mom share a bedroom and Kip sleeps in the living room. Kip should be here soon. Mom visits me every afternoon, but then she leaves about three, because she has to go home and make something for supper for Dani and Kip and then she goes to work. And then Kip comes a little after four and he stays until they serve me supper. Kip graduated from high school in June. I went, and when they called his name I clapped even though you weren't supposed to. Did your sister graduate from high school?"

"Evvie?" Thea said. "In June. I went to her graduation, too, but I didn't clap."

"Did she graduate from Briarton?" Gina asked. "Maybe she knows Kip."

Thea shook her head. "We just moved here a month or so ago," she said. "Evvie went to high school in Harrison."

"I've never been there," Gina said. "I went to Washington, D.C., once. And I'd like to go to Disneyland. Have you ever been to Disneyland?"

"No," Thea said.

"They have special programs for kids with cancer," Gina said. "The kid makes a wish and then they grant the wish. Mom applied for me a couple of times, but I never got to go to Disneyland. Does Sybil want to go to Disneyland?"

"Not if it costs money," Thea said, and she and Gina both laughed.

"Disneyland is kind of a kid place," Gina said. "Now, I'd really like to meet Dirk Marshall. He's on *The Forever Family*. Do you watch that?"

"I've seen it once or twice," Thea said.

"I think he's so cute," Gina said. "Here's a picture of him. I'd put it up over my bed, but they don't let us. Isn't he cute?"

Thea checked out Dirk Marshall's picture in *TV Dreamstars*. He was cute. "You're right," she said. "Look at those eyes."

"You have blue eyes, too," Gina said. "My eyes are brown. So are Kip's and Dani's. Dani is really pretty. She doesn't come to visit me very often because she hates hospitals. She says it isn't fair to expect her to spend time in them when she isn't the one who's sick. I'm talking a lot. Do you mind?"

"Not at all," Thea said. "I think you're interesting."

"Do you really?" Gina asked.

"I really do," Thea said. "I'd like to be your Friendly Visitor if you'd like it."

Gina nodded. "Maybe we could be friends, too," she said. "Marie and Bucky aren't friends with their Friendly Visitors, but that's because their Friendly Visitors are grown-ups. Could we be friends?"

"I don't see why not," Thea said. "Maybe when you're feeling up to it, you could visit me at home. You could be my Friendly Visitor for the day."

"And I could meet your sisters," Gina said. "Maybe Sybil and I could become friends, too."

"I think you'd like each other," Thea said.

"Who would like who?"

"Kip!" Gina said. "Kip, this is Thea. She's my Friendly Visitor. Thea, this is Kip, my brother."

Thea smiled. "Hi, Kip," she said. "I didn't hear you walk in."

"I walk softly," Kip said. "But I carry a big stick." He looked at Thea, who waited for him to smile, which he didn't. Eventually she stopped waiting. She would have liked to see him smile, to see if his smile rivaled Gina's. Not that he wasn't good-looking without the smile. Not as cute as Dirk Marshall, but definitely good-looking, with dark brown hair and brown eyes.

"Gina's been telling me all about your family," Thea said. "We only met a few minutes ago, but I feel like I know all of you."

"Lucky girl," Kip said, and then he turned his attention to Gina. "Hi there, pumpkinhead," he said. "How has your day been?"

"Boring," Gina said.

"Did you do your arithmetic lesson?" Kip asked.

"I tried, but I couldn't figure it out," Gina said. "It's hard when there's no one to ask. I did my English, though. I read the story in the book and I answered all the questions."

"Good," Kip said. "Did Mom help you?"

Gina shook her head. "Mom brought her checkbook and her bills," she replied. "And she said there wasn't enough money for any of them. She complained about Dani a lot. She said Dani got caught shoplifting and the store was making her pay for all the stuff she stole. She said she wished Dani would steal from cheaper stores and that if she got into trouble like this one more time then she'd just let her go to jail and see how Dani liked that."

"I'll talk to Dani tonight," Kip said. "I don't really think she wants to go to jail."

"I bet the food in jail is even worse than it is here," Gina said.

"Speaking of which, I brought you a doughnut," Kip said. He whipped out a paper bag and handed it to his sister. "Chocolate creme. Your favorite."

Gina looked in the bag. "Maybe later," she said. "I'm not really hungry right now."

"Later, then," Kip said. "All right. If you feel up to it, why don't we start on that arithmetic lesson."

"Not while Thea is here," Gina said. "Thea's going to be my friend, too, Kip. And she'll visit me and then you won't have to come here so much."

"I like coming here," Kip said. "Are you going to deprive me of that, pumpkinhead?"

"Nobody likes coming here," Gina said.

"True," Kip said. "I like seeing you. And if the only place to see you is here, then coming here isn't so bad. Is that honest enough for you?"

Gina nodded.

"So let's get to work on that arithmetic lesson," Kip said.

"Can Thea help?" Gina asked.

"Sure," Kip said. "How's your long division?"

"Fabulous," Thea replied. "I'm the envy of all I know."

Gina giggled, and even Kip smiled. It was half Gina's smile and it looked like it took him twice the effort.

"No arithmetic now, I'm afraid," a nurse said, walking toward Gina's bed. "I need a few minutes alone with Gina, if you don't mind."

"Of course we mind," Kip said. "But what must be must be."

"Don't go," Gina said. "You, too, Thea. Thea's my Friendly Visitor."

"I'm pleased to meet you, Thea," the nurse said. "I'm sorry for the interruption, but, Gina, honey, you know the routine."

"She could teach it to you," Kip said. "Gina, we'll be waiting outside. But as soon as we get back, it's arithmetic time."

"Okay," Gina said.

Kip and Thea walked out of the ward as the nurse pulled the curtain around Gina's bed. "I like Gina a lot," Thea said as they stood outside the room. "She's very sweet."

"She talks too much," Kip replied. "But I guess she doesn't have that many chances to talk. I hope you didn't mind all that stuff about Dani."

"That's okay," Thea said. "I've heard worse."

"Dani's going through a rough time," Kip said. "Mom works four to midnight weekdays, and she has a part-time job on weekends as well. Whatever spare time she has, she spends here. Dani's alone a lot more than she should be."

"That must be very hard on all of you," Thea said. "Your mother working so much."

"Working cuts down on her drinking," Kip replied. "So in some ways it's good. I work eight to four at the Burger Bliss. I'm the sub assistant manager. That means I'm eighteen and full time. Do you go to school?"

"Briarton High," Thea said. "I'm a junior."

"I don't remember having seen you there," Kip said.

"We just moved here," Thea replied. "We used to live in Harrison."

"Do you always visit hospitals?" Kip asked. "Is that how you get your kicks?"

"No," Thea said. "This is my first time."

"Well, I hope it isn't your last," Kip declared. "Gina seems to like you."

"She said this was her fourth time in the hospital," Thea said. "I can't imagine what that must be like."

"It's hell," Kip said. "Maybe a little bit worse than hell."

"You must all be looking forward to when she gets home," Thea said.

"Gina isn't coming home," Kip replied.

"You mean you're moving?" Thea asked. "Gina said your apartment was small."

Kip stared at Thea. "I mean Gina's going to die here," he said. "She's never going to get well enough to come back home."

Oh, God, Thea thought. Nicky, what have you gotten me into?

"You didn't know?" Kip said. "Nobody told you?"

"No," Thea said. "Mrs. Chambers just said there was a high cure-rate. Sixty percent. And Gina certainly didn't say. Does she know?"

Kip shrugged. "Probably," he said. "She hasn't brought it up, at least not with me, and probably not with Mom, either. I would have heard about it if she had. That doesn't mean she doesn't know, just that she doesn't want to talk about it. So don't you mention it, either, okay?"

"Sure," Thea said. "I never would. How can you know? Did the doctors tell you?"

"Doctors don't say things like die anymore," Kip replied. "They say there's no point continuing treatments and we should prepare ourselves for the worst and it's probably just a matter of months. This is Gina's fourth bout with cancer. The first three times the treatments put her in remission. This time, they haven't. Remission is life, no matter how short it lasts. No remission is death, which lasts forever I'm told. It's that simple."

"No," Thea said. "It's not simple."

"You're right," Kip said. "It's not simple at all. So do you still want to be Gina's Friendly Visitor?"

Thea thought about it, while trying to look as though she weren't. She'd never known anyone who'd died before, not even grandparents, let alone someone Sybil's age. And what if that were Sybil lying on the hospital bed while they all waited out the time until she died. How would Thea ever be able to survive? No wonder Kip didn't smile.

"I like Gina," she said. "And Gina seems happy to have a Friendly Visitor."

"Happier than I've seen her in a while," Kip said. "Maybe you can talk her into eating that doughnut."

"I'll give it a try," Thea said. "The doughnut, I mean. I'll stick with being Gina's Friendly Visitor."

"Thank you," Kip said. "In return, I promise we'll never send you down to bail Dani out."

Thea nodded. "It's a deal," she said.

The nurse walked through the door and smiled at them. "I'm all done," she said. "And Gina's eager to get on with your visit."

"We're eager, too," Kip said. "Come on, Thea. Let's teach the kid some math while we have the chance."

CHAPTER FOUR

"Tell me some more about your family," Gina said as Thea stretched in the chair by her bed.

"We're not through with your spelling lesson yet," Thea replied. Two weeks had passed since the girls had met, and Thea had settled into a comfortable routine of visiting Gina on Mondays and Thursdays. This was a Thursday visit, and Thea wasn't about to let Gina get away with anything.

"I've spelled every word in the dictionary," Gina declared. "Twice. Come on, Thea. I want to hear some more about your sisters. Do you think they'll visit me sometime?"

"Not if you don't finish your spelling," Thea said. "*Desperate.*"

"What?"

"Spell *desperate* and use it in a sentence," Thea said. "Remember? The same way you spelled all the other words in the dictionary."

"You mean incorrectly?" Kip asked. Thea could never get over how quietly Kip slipped in by Gina's bedside, or how happy Gina was to see him.

"Gina's been spelling well today," Thea informed him. "When I can get her to concentrate on it."

"The word was *desperate*," Kip declared. "I know the feeling. Come on, Gina. Spell it for the Kipper."

Gina and Kip laughed the intimate laugh of an old family joke. Thea thought of all the jokes she and Evvie had shared, and felt that little lurch of loneliness she'd come to associate with thoughts of Evvie. They wrote pretty often but it wasn't the same as being together all the time.

"*Desperate*," Gina said. "D-E-S-P-A-R-A-T-E. I am desperate to get out of here."

"I'm desperate for you to learn how to spell," Kip said. "It's P-E-R, pumpkin."

"E-R, A-R," Gina said, and then she giggled. "I know a lot more about E-R than I do about A-R," she said.

"I'll put you in the E.R. if you don't start paying attention," Thea said, and was gratified when Gina and Kip both laughed. "All right. Now that you know how to spell *desperate*, how about giving *destruction* a chance?"

"*Desperate, destruction*," Kip said. "That's one upbeat spelling lesson."

"I'm just following orders," Thea said. "Your mother left a list of words for Gina to spell. She didn't tell me to make them happy words."

"I can spell *destruction*," Gina said. "D-E-S-T-R-U-C-T-I-O-N. *Destruction*. I witnessed the destruction of my family."

"Gina!" Thea said.

"What?" Gina replied. "Did I spell it wrong?"

"I think Thea prefers happier sentences," Kip said. "I witnessed the destruction of disease and poverty."

"I witnessed the destruction of my entire nervous system ever since I met the two of you," Thea said, closing the notebook containing the spelling list. "You're worse than Sybil."

"How is Sybil bad?" Gina asked. She curled up in her bed, and Thea had the sensation of telling her a bedtime story. She used to make up stories for Sybil, years ago. They were mostly half-remembered versions of the stories Evvie had made up for her. Claire always refused to listen.

"Sybil is the world's greatest speller," Thea declared. "I mean it. She can spell anything. Only spelling bores her, because when you can do it as easily as she can, it's hard to be interested. So she makes up spellings."

"You mean she puts her *e* before her *i*?" Kip asked.

"Nothing that simple," Thea said. "She spells words backward. Correctly, but backward. Or she spells words one letter off, so *desperate* would start E-F-T, and then go on. If you wrote down how she spelled it, you'd see what she was doing, and she always got the word right, but she'd go so fast, it was hard to keep track."

"It sounds serious," Kip declared. "How did you handle it?"

"I stopped spelling with her," Thea said. "We all stopped testing her, but I won't even ask her how to spell a word anymore when I'm writing something. I'd rather find the dictionary, which moves around a lot in my family, than ask Sybil's help in spelling."

"Sybil's my favorite," Gina said. "She's my age, Kip."

"I know," Kip said. "You've told me that twenty-five times."

"Is she your favorite?" Gina asked Thea.

"I don't have a favorite," Thea said. "They're all my sisters, so I love them all."

"I wish I had sisters," Gina said.

"You have a sister," Kip replied. "Remember?"

"I just wish I had more of them," Gina said. "Sisters like Thea has. I wish I had a sister just like Thea. Sometimes I wish I could be Sybil and have three big sisters and a mother and a father and not be stuck in bed all the time."

Thea didn't know what to say. Even on Sybil's worst day, she had things a thousand times better than Gina.

"Where do I fit in, then?" Kip asked. "With all those sisters and parents?"

"You'd be my brother, anyway," Gina replied. "I can have a brother, can't I, Thea? Even if you don't?"

"You can have as many brothers as you'd like," Thea said. "I always wanted a brother. When all you have is sisters, a brother sounds pretty terrific."

"We finally agree on something," Kip said. "I'm stuck with sisters, when what I really wanted was a brother or two."

"You'd rather have a brother than me?" Gina asked.

"See," Kip declared. "Now you know how it feels. No, pumpkin, you I'd keep. Dani was the one I wanted to change. All she'd have to do is drop her *i* and become Dan."

"Thea's sisters all have girl names," Gina said. "Sybil's my favorite name."

"I'm partial to Gina myself," Kip said. "And Irving."

"Is Kip short for something?" Thea asked.

"Like Kipling?" Kip said. "No, it's a nickname. Officially I'm Paul Junior, which is a joke, given Paul Senior. My mother picked up Kip from a soap opera. She thought it sounded classy. When I go to college, I figure I'll become Paul without the junior."

"I didn't know you were going to go to college," Thea said. She felt better hearing it, and then she felt like a snob.

"Kip's going to go to college in New York," Gina declared.

"Shouldn't you have started already?" Thea asked. "Evvie's been gone for a couple of weeks now."

"I'm not going this semester," Kip said, and Thea realized from his tone that she had asked a stupid question. Kip was staying until Gina died. She knew, if she had asked him that question privately, that would have been his answer.

"Kip likes his job too much," Gina said. "He's sub assistant manager at Burger Bliss. He got a raise and everything."

"Right," Kip said. "I now earn more than minimum wage."

"I want to hear a story," Gina said. "One about your sisters, Thea."

"What kind of story?" Thea asked. "A true one or a made-up one?"

"True," Gina said. "Only babies like made-up ones. Tell me about you and your sisters when you were twelve, like me and Sybil. How old was everybody else then?"

"Evvie was fourteen, and Claire was ten, and you and Sybil were eight," Thea replied. "Let's see. I think we were living in an apartment that year, not a very nice place."

"What wasn't nice about it?" Gina asked.

"It was small and kind of ratty," Thea said. "It seems to me that was when I was twelve. We all hated that apartment so much."

"Why were you living in a small, ratty apartment?" Kip asked.

"Because we couldn't afford a big, ratty one," Thea said. "I'd think that would be pretty obvious."

"Don't you have money?" Kip asked. "You act like you do."

"We mostly have money," Thea said. "That was a bad year. Sometimes my father's investments don't work out, and then things aren't so great. But then he puts a new deal together, and the next thing you know we're rich again." She realized she was revealing family secrets and felt a twinge of disloyalty.

"We're always poor," Gina said. "I think I'd like to be rich sometimes."

"I'd like to be rich all the time," Kip declared. "The way I thought Thea was."

"Sorry to disillusion you," Thea said.

"I still want a story about when you were twelve," Gina said.

"When I was twelve, I still liked to play make-believe games," Thea said. Now that she thought about it, she liked them most that year, in that terrible apartment. They all did. That was the year they made-believe they were anyone and anyplace, just as long as they could be somewhere else for as long as the game lasted. Thea suspected even Megs liked make-believe that year. "My favorite game was Little Women. You know, from the book. There were four sisters in that, and I was one of four sisters. I always wanted to be Jo."

"Who did Sybil want to be?" Gina asked.

"Sybil didn't have much of a say in the matter," Thea said. "She was only eight, so she got last pick. Claire always insisted on being Amy, because Amy married money. And then Sybil would say she wanted to be Meg, because Meg was practical and good with money, and besides, she was the oldest, and Sybil was tired of being the youngest. She wanted a chance to boss us around. You must know how that feels, Gina."

"Did Sybil get to be Meg?" Gina asked. "It must be funny being the oldest when you're the youngest."

"No, we wouldn't let her," Thea said. "Because if Sybil was Meg, then Evvie would have had to be Beth, and Claire and I wouldn't let her be Beth because . . ." She stopped, realizing that they wouldn't let Evvie be Beth because Beth died, and they couldn't deal with Evvie dying even in a make-believe game.

"Because why?" Gina asked.

"Because Beth's a wimp," Kip said. "You know the kind. She always does her spelling assignments and never complains about them."

"Yuck," Gina said. "So Sybil had to be Beth?"

Thea nodded. "When I played Little Women just with Sybil, though, I let her be Meg," she replied. "Sybil was very good at bossing me around."

One of the nurses walked over to Gina's bed. "I hate to break up this party, but we need Gina for some tests," she said.

"Should we wait outside?" Kip asked.

The nurse shook her head. "It's going to take a while, and Gina will be pretty tired when we're through," she declared. "Why don't you make an early day of it this time, and you can visit with Gina tomorrow."

"I'll be back on Monday," Thea said. "I'll see if I can get Sybil to come."

Gina's face lit up. "Do you think she would?" she asked. "I want to meet her so much."

"I'll ask," Thea said. She smiled at Gina, and then bent down and gave her a kiss. "You take care, all right."

"I will," Gina said. " 'Bye, Thea. 'Bye, Kip."

" 'Bye, pumpkinhead," Kip said. He kissed his sister, and walked out with Thea.

"Thank you," Thea said to him as they walked down the corridor. "For rescuing me from that story about Little Women."

"Beth was a wimp," Kip declared. "She probably died asking for another spelling assignment."

"I forget sometimes that Gina is dying," Thea said. "She seems so lively, so vital."

"You should have known her when she was in remission," Kip said. "You couldn't keep her down. Now I look at her . . . Well, she puts out a lot of effort when you're there."

"She doesn't have to," Thea said.

"She doesn't do it consciously," Kip said. "It's good. She gets excited about your visits."

"Maybe I should come more often, then," Thea said.

Kip shook his head. "Don't start something you can't continue," he said. "You've been to see her what, four times? That's okay. That's no big deal. After ten or twelve or twenty times, you might not want to see her quite so often. And then Gina will get used to your visits, come to expect them, and you'll feel like you're letting her down if you don't see her so often, then you'll feel guilty and she'll feel bad and then you'll stop coming altogether. Twice a week is fine. Once a week is okay, too."

"You really are a cynic," Thea said. "I like Gina. I like her as a human being. I like spending time with her."

"Do you like watching her die?" Kip asked.

"I've never known Gina when she wasn't dying," Thea replied. "The Gina I see now is the only Gina I know."

Kip stood for a moment, turned around, and faced Thea. "I'm sorry," he said. "I underestimated you."

Thea tried to keep from blushing.

"It's just that you're pretty, and you dress well, and there's an air about you," Kip said. "Something rich and soft."

"And that's worse than hard and poor?" Thea asked. "You'd trust hard and poor more?"

Kip grinned. "I'd feel more at home with it," he replied.

Thea smiled back. "Do you think I'll stop coming because Dani has?" she asked.

Kip shook his head. "You're nothing like Dani," he said. "Dani's wild, and all this is making her mean. Not that I blame her. I'd like to be wild and mean myself."

"You?" Thea said. "The sub assistant manager of Burger Bliss?"

Kip brushed his hair back off his forehead. "Inside I am wild and mean," he declared. "Inside I'm a lot of things I don't show when I'm with Gina."

"Like what?" Thea asked. They were at the hospital door, but Thea didn't want the conversation to stop. She wasn't sure whether it was because she'd been walking with Kip or because she was more accustomed to the place, but this was the first time she hadn't felt lost getting from Gina's ward to the front lobby.

"Like angry," Kip said, opening the door for Thea to walk through. He followed her out, and they continued to stand together. It was a perfect end-of-September day, the leaves turning, and the sky pure blue. The hospital was on a hill, and from the front door, Thea could see Briarton laid out below. Gina's bed had a view of the town, and Thea had wondered if she liked that, or if it bothered her to know there was a world out there with normal healthy kids.

"You have a lot to be angry about," Thea replied.

"It's not that simple," Kip said. "Where do you live?"

"On Oak Street," Thea said.

"Really?" Kip said. "I would have thought you'd live in one of the newer developments. Or is your family having a not-rich stage right now?"

"My mother wanted a house she could renovate," Thea said. "So we found a beautiful old Victorian that needs a lot of work. She's been working on it since we moved in, but once she's through, it's going to be perfect. I really hope we'll stay there forever."

"You don't sound like that's going to happen," Kip said.

"We've moved around a lot," Thea replied. "Where do you live?"

"North Street," Kip said. "In a ratty, small apartment. How about if I walk you home?"

"That's fine," Thea said. "But won't it be out of your way?"

"I know some shortcuts," Kip said. "And I have some extra time. Dani won't be expecting me for another hour."

"All right," Thea said. They started walking away from the hospital, going downhill. Thea always liked that part of the walk home. It was easier than the walk to the hospital, with the last couple of hundred yards always feeling as though they were on a forty-five-degree angle. "What's not that simple about your anger?"

"Do you know much about alcoholism?" Kip asked.

"No," Thea said.

"Well, I know a lot about it," Kip declared. "My mother's an alcoholic, although she manages to hold on to a job. She never drinks before going to work, which is why this four-to-midnight job is so good for her."

"That must be hard on all of you," Thea said.

"You make adjustments," Kip replied. "Everybody has a role. You have a part to play and you play it. One kid might take care of everybody else in the family. One kid is the scapegoat, the troublemaker. One kid runs away, another could make jokes. Only my family got everything screwed up."

"I don't see that," Thea said. "You're clearly the grown-up, and Dani's the troublemaker. I don't know which one Gina is, but maybe that's because she's been sick."

"Gina's sickness is the problem," Kip said. "You have to remember, Gina's been sick forever. Before then, we had one set of roles, and ever since then, we've had to shift those roles around. Dani used to be the jokemaker. When she was little, she could make the trees smile. And I was the runaway. I stayed away from home as much as I could. I was always sleeping over at a friend's house, even if I wasn't invited, which half the time I wasn't. I felt bad, because I knew my parents were fighting, and things were worse when I wasn't there, but most of me figured that

I was their lookout. I didn't even care enough to protect Dani and Gina."

"But then Gina got sick," Thea said.

"Right," Kip said. "She got sick and my father pulled out. He became the runaway, which was really cheating. My mother was already drinking, but after that, she drank a lot more, and Dani stopped making jokes, and I had to become the grown-up. That's what makes me mad. I don't like being this responsible. I'm not a responsible sort of person. I like hiding from things, not having to deal with them. You think I like having to put off college?"

"No," Thea said.

"I went through a lot to get the scholarships I needed, and the loans," Kip declared. "I begged on paper. I begged on the phone. Once I begged in person. I hated it. But then Gina got sick again, and the treatments didn't help, and I knew it was just a matter of time, of months, and I had to tell all those people I'd begged from that college was going to have to wait. My life is on hold until Gina dies. That means part of me wants Gina to die, so I can get on with things."

"You don't want Gina to die," Thea said. "I've seen you with her. You love her too much."

"Part of me wants her to die," Kip said. "We all do. Maybe even Gina wants it a little."

"Well, I don't," Thea said. "And I'm going to keep hoping for a miracle. People go into remission unexpectedly. People get cured unexpectedly, too. That's what I want."

"Fine," Kip said. "But do me a favor."

"What?" Thea asked. She wasn't ready yet to grant Kip one without finding out what it was first.

"Don't fill Gina up with false hopes," Kip said.

"About her getting well?" Thea asked.

"About everything," Kip said. "Don't tell her she's going to visit your family, when she's never going to leave the hospital again. And don't tell her that precious sister Sybil of yours is going to come for a visit, unless you know for sure she really will. Gina doesn't have anything, so she hopes for things a little more than most people. All she's going to talk about for the next three days is Sybil's visit."

"I can't guarantee that Sybil will visit," Thea said.

"That's my point," Kip said. "You can't guarantee, but Gina's going to count on it. And I don't want her to be disappointed again."

"I was going to say that I couldn't guarantee it, but I was sure Sybil would come," Thea declared angrily. "We do things for each other in my family. Not because we're scared or because of roles we play, but because we want to. And when Sybil hears how important it is to me, she'll come visit Gina."

"I sure hope so," Kip said. "I don't want to be the one to have to explain to Gina why the legendary Sybil isn't there."

"You won't have to," Thea said. "That I do guarantee."

CHAPTER FIVE

"**I** don't see why we have to do this," Claire grumbled. "Wouldn't it be easier just to paint?"

"Easier isn't necessarily better," Meg replied. "I don't want to cover this grime with another coat of paint. I want to clean it off, and then paint."

"Fine," Claire said. "Then you do it. Why should I have to?"

"Because this is a family project," Nick said. "And you're part of this family, Claire. As long as you live under this roof, you have responsibilities."

"I'll move, then," Claire said.

"Think of it as historic grime," Sybil said. "Filth of a hundred years."

"If this dirt could talk," Thea said. "The wars. The anguish."

"The sex?" Claire asked.

"I don't know how much sex the dining room saw," Meg said. "I don't even want to know how much sex the dining room saw."

Everyone laughed. Thea put her pair of rubber gloves on, grabbed a bucket of soapy water, and dropped in a sponge. She had the left-side wall to clean, and the sooner she got to it, the quicker the job would be done.

Sybil followed Thea's lead and was soon hard at work on her wall. Meg scrubbed away as well, and even Claire got into the rhythm, and cleaned. Thea noticed though that Claire took frequent breaks to check on her fingernails. Nicky, who hated working with his hands, provided the fresh buckets of soapy water.

Thea climbed a ladder, and scrubbed close to the ceiling. She felt it wouldn't hurt to have some distance between herself and Sybil when she made her request.

"Do you have any plans for Monday afternoon, Sybil?" she asked, trying to sound casual.

"I don't know," Sybil said. "Megs, do I have any plans?"

"Not that I know of," Meg replied. "Why?"

"Because Thea just asked me," Sybil said.

"I know that," Meg said. "Why did Thea ask?"

"I don't know," Sybil said. "Why don't you ask her?"

Thea was afraid if she laughed too hard she'd knock the bucket off the ladder. "I asked because, well, it's kind of hard to explain."

"That means it has something to do with money," Claire said. "Everything else is easy to explain."

"If only that were true," Nick said. "Anyone need a fresh bucket?"

"I do," Sybil said, and Nicky brought it over to her. "What's up, Thea?"

"Thea's up," Claire said. "On the ladder."

"If you'd all stop with the editorial comments, I'd tell you," Thea said.

"You have my undivided attention," Nick declared.

Unfortunately, it wasn't Nicky's attention that Thea wanted. She sighed, scrubbed, and thought about how to put it. "You know Gina, the girl I've been visiting?" she began.

"That poor child," Meg said. "How is she, Thea?"

"She's okay," Thea said. "I mean, she's dying, so I guess she isn't okay, but she isn't dead yet, so I guess she's okay." She scowled. None of this was coming out the way she wanted.

"I never want to be sick," Sybil declared.

"Nobody wants to be sick," Claire said. "Unless you have a test you didn't study for."

"That's not what I mean," Sybil said. "I mean I hate everything about sickness and hospitals."

"You don't know anything about sickness and hospitals," Claire said.

"That's right," Thea said. "You might like them once you got to know them."

Everyone laughed. Thea felt like drowning in dirty suds water. "I could use a new bucket," she said.

"You could use a new brain," Claire said.

"Stop that," Meg said. "Now, Thea, what do you want to tell us about Gina?"

Thea smiled down at her mother. Trust Megs to figure

out how Thea should explain her problem. "I tell Gina stories about us," Thea said. "About the family. She has a brother and a sister, but she likes to hear about all of us."

"We know she has a brother," Claire said. "All you ever talk about is Kip."

"I do not," Thea said. She hadn't been aware of talking about him at all. She'd probably casually mentioned him once, and Claire had remembered because Claire remembered everything having to do with males.

"Yes, you do," Sybil said. "It's always Kip was here or Kip said that. You talk about him almost as much as Evvie talks about Sam."

"You're both crazy," Thea said, feeling very uncomfortable. "Anyway, that's beside the point. Gina has a sister, too, Dani, but she never comes to visit."

"Dani Dozier?" Claire asked. "She's Gina's sister?"

"Yeah," Thea said. "You know her?"

"Everyone knows her," Claire replied. "She's really wild."

Thea couldn't tell whether Claire approved or disapproved. She wasn't about to find out, either. "Gina is nothing like Dani," she said.

"She couldn't be," Claire pointed out. "Stuck in a hospital bed all the time."

"That's what I wanted to say," Thea replied. "Gina is stuck there, and she has heard all about you, and she really wants to meet you. Sybil, I mean."

"Why does she want to meet me?" Sybil asked. "I don't know her."

"If you knew her, she wouldn't have to meet you," Claire said. "Nicky, if I have to do this, could you at least bring me another bucket."

"I never got mine, either," Thea said.

"Sorry," Nick said. "I was engrossed in your conversation." He left for the kitchen, and they all paused until he brought in two fresh buckets. Thea noticed, not for the first time, how everything in their family seemed to stop when Nicky left the room.

"Thanks," Thea said as he handed her the bucket. She rinsed her sponge out, and began to scrub again. "She wants to meet you, Sybil, because you're both twelve years old. That's all. I've told her all about us, and frankly, her life is pretty miserable. I mean, it would be even if she wasn't sick. Her father walked out years ago, her mother drinks, and they don't have any money."

"Poor girl," Meg said.

"All that and cancer, too," Claire said. "She must be a bundle of laughs."

"She's very nice," Thea said. "And Kip is also." She blushed as soon as she said his name, and waited for the teasing to begin. Only it didn't.

"You know, when I suggested the volunteer work, I never thought you'd be dealing with families like that," Nick declared. "That wasn't at all what I wanted for you."

"It was Mrs. Chambers's idea," Thea said. "She matched me with Gina. They all love Gina at the hospital."

"I suppose," Nick said. "Still, next time, maybe I'll think a little harder before making a suggestion."

Thea knew it had been more an order than a suggestion, but she wasn't about to bring it up. "Anyway, Sybil," she said. "I told Gina you'd visit her, so she could meet you."

"Oh, Thea," Sybil said. "I don't want to."

"It won't be for long," Thea said. "It isn't like you have to see her twice a week, like I do. Just come with me Monday afternoon for a half hour or so. It would mean so much to her."

"Sure, that's fine if she's really dying," Sybil said. "But what if she hangs on, and she expects me to visit her again and again?"

"Sybil!" Meg said sharply.

"Thea didn't have any right to say I'd come," Sybil said. "I don't care if she goes to the hospital and visits some crummy sick person. But that doesn't mean I have to."

"I'm very sorry to hear you talk that way," Meg said. "I thought you had some compassion in you, Sybil, for those who need it."

"You mean she sounds like me," Claire said. "I'm on your side, Sybil. Thea is always volunteering people for stuff like that. She figures just because she likes playing Lady Bountiful, we all should."

Thea considered dumping her bucket of water on Claire, but Megs was in the way, and Megs was her ally. "It's just one afternoon," she said. "Gina's dying, Sybil. She could be dead next week. I'm asking you to give up one hour of your life for someone who's dying."

"It isn't just an hour of my life," Sybil said. "Scrubbing this dining room is giving up an hour of my life, and you haven't heard me complain about that. But I hate hospitals. They scare me. And I wouldn't know what to say to her, and she probably won't like me, anyway. I know the way you talk about us, Thea. It's like we're angels or something. How do you think I'll feel if I go to visit this dying kid, and she takes one look at me and hates me?"

"You'll still feel a lot better than she does," Thea declared. "And besides, she won't hate you. She's just a normal kid, Sybil. She reads *TV Dreamstars* magazine."

"I certainly don't read *TV Dreamstars* magazine," Sybil said. "What kind of an idiot do you take me for?"

"A selfish one, apparently," Thea said. Where was Evvie when she needed her. Evvie could talk Sybil into anything.

"You're the one who's being selfish," Sybil said. "Trying to make me do something I don't want to do."

"That's right, Thea," Claire said. "You think now that Evvie's away, you can boss us around."

"This has nothing to do with Evvie, and nothing to do with bossing," Thea said, although she had just been wishing that Evvie were there to boss Sybil around. "This has to do with being kind."

"I don't want to be kind," Sybil said. "I'm not a kind person."

"Megs!" Thea cried. "Nicky!"

"Sybil, I think you're behaving badly," Meg declared. "Even if you aren't a kind person, you can still spare a couple of hours to bring cheer into someone's life. I'm going to be very disappointed in you if you don't go."

Thea smiled. Megs had come through, and now Nicky was sure to. They always agreed on the important things.

"Nicky, do I have to go?" Sybil asked. Thea could tell Sybil was making a last-ditch appeal she didn't expect to win.

"I'm not so sure it's a good idea for Sybil to go," Nick declared.

"Nicky!" Thea shrieked. She shook the ladder so much some drops of water fell on Megs's head.

"Thea!" Meg said. "Nicholas! What is going on with this family?"

"We hate scrubbing walls," Claire said. "This is what happens when you make us scrub walls."

"You really mean I don't have to go, Nicky?" Sybil asked. "Oh, thank you."

"Hear me out, Daisy," Nick said. "These are not desirable people. These are definitely not the sort of people we want our daughters to spend time with."

"She's a dying girl," Meg said.

"She's a dying girl from a trashy family," Nick said. "Everything Thea has told us about them is bad. Desertion, alcoholism, no money. This Kip person Thea keeps talking about. What does he do?"

"He's sub assistant manager at the Burger Bliss," Thea said.

"Exactly," Nick said. "It's bad enough Thea has to spend time with them, but I guess it's too late to prevent that. Claire, I want you to promise me you won't have anything to do with that other sister, what's-her-name, Dani."

"I give you my solemn word, Nicky," Claire said. "I wouldn't want to have anything to do with her, anyway. She's cheap."

"I'm not surprised to hear it," Nick said. "Thea, I don't want Mrs. Chambers to get the wrong idea about you, so you can keep seeing Gina twice a week. But that's the only contact I want any member of this family to have with her or her family."

"Nicky, you are so wrong," Thea said. "They're not like that. And besides, the only ones I ever see are Gina and Kip. And you'd like Kip, Nicky. He's going to go to college as soon as he can. He's just working at the Burger Bliss to help out while Gina's . . . while she's still sick."

"You mean until she dies," Sybil said. "I hate the idea of someone my age dying of something. It's bad enough getting cramps."

"Perhaps when Gina is no longer well enough to appreciate your visits, you could ask Mrs. Chambers to fix you up with someone more appropriate," Nick said.

"Disease doesn't require a pedigree," Thea declared. "People get sick. Nice people. Nice people come from bad families. It isn't like your family was so great."

"My family is not at issue here," Nick said. "Nor do I appreciate that tone of voice when you're talking about things you don't understand."

"I understand why you don't want to visit this Gina person, Sybil and I don't blame you, but I think I'll go with Thea on Monday," Claire said.

"What?" Thea said.

"You heard me," Claire said. "Hospitals don't scare me. I don't mind going. I know I'm not as exciting as Sybil, but I guess I'll have to do."

"I don't see any reason for you to go, Claire," Nick said. "And I'd prefer it if you didn't."

"I know," Claire said. "That's why I've decided to go. We can walk together after school, all right, Thea?"

"Fine," Thea said. "I know Gina will be pleased to meet you. The only reason she wants to meet Sybil is because Sybil is her age."

"What's going on here?" Nick asked. "Claire, you've never volunteered to do a nice thing in your life."

Claire shrugged. "I'm not being nice," she said. "Just curious. I want to see this Kip with my own eyes. I figure if he has Dani for a sister, and you're so dead set against him, he's probably worth a look."

Thea scowled. It was just like Claire to decide to chase Kip. And how was Kip supposed to deal with a beautiful avaricious fourteen-year-old like Claire?

"Kip will be there?" Sybil asked.

"Maybe," Thea said. "Maybe not."

Claire laughed. "Kip is always there," she said. "You've got to start paying more attention, Sybil. Even Thea says interesting things sometimes."

"I am sick and tired of your attitude, Claire," Meg said. "Yours also, Sybil. It isn't going to kill either of you to visit a sick child. As a matter of fact, I think I'll visit, too."

"Not on Monday," Claire said. "Monday's my day to visit."

"Daisy, I understand that you like to help the less fortunate," Nick said. "That's one of the things I love about you. But in this case, why not leave bad enough alone? Thea, keep visiting. Claire, go if you must, but just the once. Daisy, if you have the time to do volunteer work, fine. Ask Mrs. Chambers. I'm sure she'll be delighted with your assistance. But I don't want any more involvement with Gina's family than that. Have I made myself clear?"

"You're a great one for helping the less fortunate if it serves your purposes," Thea said. "You were the one who made me do this volunteer work in the first place. Why? You thought I'd be fluffing pillows only for rich sick people?"

"I don't care for your attitude, Thea," Nick said.

"I don't care if you do care," Thea said. She was trembling so hard she had to hold on to the ladder.

"This has all been a terrible mistake," Meg said. "I thought we could all do something together, clean the dining room, the way a family should. I see I was wrong. If anything is going to get done in this house, I'll have to do it alone. Fine. I want all of you out of here. Do you hear me? I want you out of here right now."

"I'll stay, Megs," Sybil said. "I like helping out."

"Out!" Meg said. "This instant!"

Thea climbed down the ladder. She couldn't understand why Megs should be mad at her. They were the only two who agreed. She carried the bucket down with her, and left it on the floor, by Megs's side. Megs did not smile at her as Thea stood there.

"Out," Meg said. "And I don't want any of you anywhere near this dining room until I tell you to come in."

Even Claire was silent. She filed out of the room with Thea and Sybil. They climbed the stairs slowly, trying to hear any conversation between Nicky and Megs. If there was any, it was whispered.

"I've never seen her that mad," Thea said, walking into Claire and Sybil's room with them. It no longer mattered that she was angry with them. This was no time to be alone.

"I thought she was going to start crying," Sybil said. She looked like she might cry as well. "I never meant to make her that mad."

"It wasn't just you," Thea said. "It was all of us. Except maybe me."

"Sure," Claire said. "Little Miss Perfect would never do anything to upset Big Miss Perfect."

"You make me sick," Thea said. "And you do, too, Sybil."

"I'm sorry," Sybil said. "I'll go with you if you still want me to."

"Congratulations," Claire said. "You finally bullied Sybil into doing what you want her to."

"I'm glad," Thea said. "If it took bullying, fine. She's going to make a very sweet girl feel a little bit happier. It's about time Sybil agreed. If she'd agreed when I first asked her, none of this would have happened."

"If she'd agreed, when you first asked her, we'd still be scrubbing the dining room walls," Claire said. "I'd rather be here. Thanks, Syb."

"You're welcome, I guess," Sybil said. "Is it scary in the hospital, Thea? Are there a lot of dead people all over?"

"I haven't seen a dead one yet," Thea told her. "It's just a few sick kids in a big room. It's kind of like that room we had in Harrison, only nicer. And some of the kids are bald. That's all."

"Is Gina bald?" Sybil asked.

Thea shook her head.

"The hell with Gina," Claire said. "Is Kip bald?"

Sybil laughed. Thea was torn between laughing and throttling Claire. Laughing won out.

"What do you think they're doing down there?" Sybil asked.

Claire checked the clock. "By now?" she said. "By now, they're probably showing the dining room some sex," she said.

"Claire!" Thea said.

"Wanna bet?" Claire asked.

"Absolutely not," Thea said.

"I'd rather they were having sex there than fighting," Sybil said. "Wouldn't you, Thea?"

"Thea doesn't like to think about sex," Claire said. "All she likes is love."

"Love's what's important," Thea said.

"Yeah, but sex is what's fun," Claire replied.

"I don't care about either one of them," Sybil declared. "Just as long as I never end up dying in a hospital."

"You won't," Thea promised her. "Not as long as I'm around to protect you."

CHAPTER SIX

"I think I've changed my mind," Sybil muttered as they stood outside the hospital door. "Do I have to go in?"

"You promised," Thea declared. "It really isn't so bad in there, Sybil. You won't mind once you get used to the place."

"Why can't you and Claire go without me?" Sybil asked. "Hospitals are scary. They're full of sick people and dead bodies."

"You'll be a dead body if you don't move it," Claire said. "Come on, Sybil. The sooner we get in there, the sooner we can leave."

"You're going to owe me one," Sybil declared. "A big one, Thea."

"And I'll pay you back, I promise," Thea replied. "Come on. Gina's going to be so thrilled."

"And I'm going to be so sick," Sybil said, but she followed Thea through the corridors. Her complexion, Thea noticed, had turned pale green, but she needed hardly any pushing from her two older sisters. Claire, on the other hand, looked right at home. She cast appraising glances at every man she saw, and gave more careful looks to the male doctors. The men looked back at her. Thea wondered what Claire would be like if she weren't so beautiful, and then realized she wouldn't be Claire. Claire *was* her beauty. She was all magnificent exterior.

"This is Gina's ward," Thea whispered. "Come on. Let's go over so you can meet her."

"Thrillsville," Claire muttered, but she led Sybil to the bed that Thea pointed them to.

"Gina, hi, how are you?" Thea asked.

"I'm okay," Gina said. Thea noticed how listless she looked, and how small in comparison to Sybil. This was the Gina who was dying, not the twelve-year-old Gina Thea was used to.

"I brought you some visitors," Thea declared. "Gina, I want you to meet two of my sisters, Claire and Sybil."

Gina pulled herself up in her bed, and Thea rearranged her pillows to give her some support. "Really?" Gina said. "They're really Claire and Sybil?"

"What do you think, that she'd hire ringers?" Claire asked. "Thea doesn't have that kind of imagination. Hi, Gina. I'm Claire."

"And I'm Sybil," Sybil said. She extended her hand for Gina to shake. Thea noticed it was shaking, and gave Sybil five extra points for bravery.

"I can't believe you're really here," Gina said. "Thea's told me so much about you, and I've wanted to meet you, and now you're actually here."

"We wanted to meet you, too," Claire said. "Thea hasn't talked about anyone else since the two of you became friends."

Thea couldn't believe what she was hearing. Claire was being nice. Where was the catch?

"I like her so much," Gina said. "You're so lucky to have a sister like her."

"We know," Sybil said. At least Claire didn't agree. Thea was starting to worry that Claire herself had hired the ringer. "Do you have any sisters, Gina?"

Gina nodded. "One," she said. "Her name is Dani."

"I know her," Claire said. "We're not in any of the same classes, but I've seen her around school. She's very pretty."

"You really know Dani?" Gina asked.

"She probably doesn't know me," Claire said. "I'm new to the school. We move around a lot. I don't know if you know what that's like, but when you go to a lot of different schools, it pays if you figure out fast who's important and who isn't. I guessed that Dani must be important because she's so pretty and popular."

Thea balanced herself against the chair to keep from fainting.

"You have a big brother, too, don't you?" Sybil asked. "Thea's mentioned him to us."

"Kip," Gina said. "He'll be here soon. He comes every day after work to visit."

"That's great," Sybil said. "You must be happy to see him."

"I am," Gina said. "Before Thea became my Friendly Visitor, Kip was the only visitor I had. Him and my mom. Dani would come, too, but she's so busy with school and her friends. She means to come a lot, but then stuff happens, and she can't."

"She should come more often," Claire said sharply. But then she smiled at Gina. "She could check out all the handsome doctors if she did." She winked broadly.

Gina laughed and was almost herself again. It hurt Thea to see how much worse Gina was than she'd been four days earlier. Gina really was going to die. Thea began to believe what Kip kept telling her.

"I don't know why I'm babbling this way," Claire said. "I hear from Thea that Sybil's really the one you want to meet."

"We're the same age," Gina said. "But Sybil's a year ahead of me in school."

"I haven't been sick," Sybil said, looking as though she were about to be. "I guess you've had to miss a lot."

"It's okay," Gina said. "My mother brings me homework to do. Thea's been helping me with my spelling. She says you're a wonderful speller, Sybil."

"Yeah, I guess so," Sybil said. "Thea, is there a water cooler around here?"

"I'll show you where it is," Thea said. "Claire, can you entertain Gina while we're gone?"

"I'll try," Claire said. "I hear you read *TV Dreamstars*, Gina." She found the copy by Gina's bedside, and Thea left the two of them poring over it, comparing favorites.

"I feel awful," Sybil said.

"You're acting like a baby," Thea told her. "Why can't you be more like Claire. I don't believe I said that."

"It's easy for Claire," Sybil declared. "She doesn't care. She's just playing a part."

"Then you play a part, too," Thea said. "If Claire can pretend to be nice, then you can pretend to be human. You're a lot closer to it than she is."

Sybil didn't laugh. "Gina looks terrible," she said instead. "I didn't think she'd look so sick."

"I know," Thea replied. "I never saw her look this bad."

"Do you think she's going to die today?" Sybil asked. "While we're with her?"

"No," Thea said. "Gina isn't going to die today. I promise."

"How can you be so sure?" Sybil asked.

"They wouldn't have let all of us visit if Gina was that sick," Thea declared. "Look, just hang in there a few more minutes, until Kip arrives. Claire will check him out, and then she'll want to leave, too. The two of you can go home then. All right?"

"All right," Sybil said. "I really hate hospitals, Thea. Before today, I just thought I did, but now that I've been in one, I know how much I hate them."

"You'll be out of this one in half an hour," Thea said. "And then you won't have to come back until you have a baby."

"I'll adopt," Sybil replied. "I feel better now. Let's go back."

Thea and Sybil walked back to Gina's bed. Claire had made herself comfortable on it, and was telling Gina a story that Gina was obviously entranced with.

"And then Nicky said, 'That wasn't mouse poison, that was caviar!' " Claire said, and Gina burst into giggles. "Honestly, Gina. I figured if I had to make a mistake, at least I did it the right way. Think what would have happened if Nicky had served all those business people mouse poison, thinking it was caviar. But Nicky didn't see it that way at all."

"Did he punish you?" Gina asked.

Claire tossed her hair away from her eyes. Thea was struck, as she often was, by Claire's resemblance to Nicky.

"Nicky never punishes me," she said. "He always means to, but somehow he never gets around to it."

"Does your mother punish you?" Sybil asked.

"Not since I've been sick," Gina replied. "It used to drive Dani crazy. I'd do something wrong, and Mom wouldn't say anything about it. Dani says when she does something wrong, Mom really lets her have it."

"Life is so unfair," Claire said. "Isn't it, Gina?"

Gina nodded. Thea thought about just how unfair life could be, and decided to change the topic.

"So, Gina," she said. "Did you do much schoolwork this weekend?"

"No," Gina said. "I haven't felt real good since Friday."

"Are you sick?" Sybil asked. "I mean, do you have a cold or something?"

"I don't think so," Gina replied. "Kip says I'll feel better soon. And I feel better today than I did yesterday. Do you catch colds, Sybil?"

"Sybil is never sick," Claire replied. "It drives me crazy. When I was younger, I used to get all kinds of things, mumps, stuff like that, and I'd be moaning and groaning, and Sybil never caught a single germ. I'd try. I'd tell her to finish what I was eating, and I'd swap toothbrushes on her, and pillows, and she never got anything I had."

"I didn't know you did that," Sybil said. "Boy, you're mean, Claire."

"I wasn't mean, I was lonely," Claire said. "Stuck in the house alone all day with Megs. She'd try to play with me, but it was never as much fun as when you and I played. It's really neat having a younger sister, Gina. They're much better than older ones."

"I guess," Gina said. "Older brothers are nice. I love Kip."

"I always wanted an older brother," Claire said. "I would have swapped Thea if I could."

"But not Evvie," Thea said.

"I liked Evvie," Claire said.

"You don't like Thea?" Gina asked. "Why not?"

Claire laughed. "I like Thea," she said. "I just figured she'd be easier to swap. But I never wanted a kid brother. Do you have any friends with kid brothers, Gina?"

"I used to," Gina replied.

"They are the worst," Claire said. "Always being pests. Sybil was never a pest. She wouldn't always do what I wanted her to, but at least she stayed out of my way most of the time."

"I had to," Sybil said. "You would have run right over me, otherwise."

Claire laughed, and so did Gina. Thea shook her head in disbelief. Playing a part or no, Claire looked like she was born to be a Friendly Visitor.

"What's going on here?" Kip asked, walking over to the bed. "Is this a convention of NOW or something?"

"I like that," Claire said. "You couldn't mistake us for Miss America contestants?"

"Sorry," Kip said. "I was so dazzled by all the beauty, I missed the obvious. Hi, Thea. Hello, pumpkin." He bent down and gave Gina a kiss. "You're looking better today."

"I feel better," Gina said. "Thea brought her sisters. Sybil and Claire. The one on my bed is Claire, and the other one is Sybil."

Poor Sybil,. Thea thought. Reduced from goddess to the-other-one status. Not that Sybil seemed to mind. She looked instead pathetically relieved that Kip had arrived, and was clearly counting the seconds until she and Claire could make their getaway.

"Claire," Kip said. "Sybil." He gazed at both of them. "It was nice of you to come visit."

"We wanted to meet Gina," Claire said. "Thea keeps talking about her, almost like she was another sister."

Kip stared at Claire, who stared right back. Thea didn't care for that at all. "I guaranteed you a visit," she said. "But instead of one visitor, I brought two."

"Very nice of you," Kip said. "What's that in your hand, Sybil?"

"Oh, I brought something," Sybil said. "I almost forgot. Gina, I don't know if you can keep stuff like this, but I brought you some lipstick."

"Lipstick?" Thea asked. To the best of her knowledge, Sybil didn't even know what lipstick was.

"Well, some girls my age wear makeup," Sybil said. "My parents won't let me. But I thought your mother might, and you probably couldn't get out to buy any, so I got you some. It's red." She handed over the lipstick to Gina, and then grabbed it back. "It still has its price on it," she explained. She unpeeled the sticker, and gave the lipstick to Gina.

"It is red," Gina said, twisting it open. "What do you think, Kip?"

"It's lovely," he said. "Do you want to put some on?"

"Can I?" Gina asked.

"I don't see why not," Kip said.

"I wish I had a mirror," Gina said. "So I could put it on better."

"I have one," Claire said, and she whipped a mirror out of her pocketbook. She handed it to Gina, until it became obvious Gina couldn't manage both the lipstick and the mirror. Claire took the mirror back then, and held it so Gina could see her reflection.

Gina carefully applied the lipstick. It was appallingly red, and it made Gina look all the paler. "How do I look?" Gina asked. "Older?"

"Much older," Kip said. "Thank you, Sybil."

"Why are *you* thanking her?" Claire asked. "Do you intend to wear it, Kip?"

Kip and Gina both laughed. Thea could see then how much they looked alike, what Gina would have grown up to look like if things had been better.

"Dani wears makeup," Gina said. "Lots of it."

"I know," Claire said. "She wears it really well, too. Some girls just cover their faces with it, and they don't know what they're doing, but Dani wears just the right amount and colors. I wish I could do that, but Nicky and Megs say I'm too young. Next year they say."

"You don't need makeup," Kip said. "Neither does Gina. You're both natural beauties."

"Men," Claire said to Gina. "They think that's a compliment." She and Gina shared a smile.

"Uh, Claire, now that Kip's here, maybe you and Sybil should get going," Thea declared. "We don't want to tire Gina out with too much company."

"Would you like us to stay a little longer, Gina?" Claire asked.

"Thanks, Claire, but Thea's right," Kip said. "Natural beauties shouldn't get overstimulated."

"All right," Claire said with a sigh. "Come on, Sybil. We're being kicked out."

"I know," Sybil said. "I hope you like the lipstick, Gina."

"I love it," Gina said. "Thank you, Sybil. Thank you, Claire."

"You're welcome," Claire said. She gathered her things

and got up to leave. "Oh, Kip," she said. "Nicky and Megs were both saying how much they'd like to meet you, too. Why don't you come over for supper one day this week?"

"Thank you," Kip said. "Are you sure?"

"Of course I'm sure," Claire said. "Today's Monday. How's Wednesday?"

"Oh, please go, Kip," Gina said. "Then you can tell me all about their house."

Kip smiled. "Fine," he said. "I'll see you on Wednesday then."

"Great," Claire said. "Come on, Sybil. Let's give these people some peace and quiet."

"I'm coming," Sybil said, and she followed Claire out.

"That was wonderful," Gina said. "Thank you, Thea."

"You're welcome," Thea said. "They wanted to meet you, too."

"Claire is so beautiful," Gina said. "Isn't she, Kip?"

Kip nodded. "She's the most beautiful girl I've ever seen," he replied.

Thea was used to hearing that about Claire, but it annoyed her anyway. "Sybil's beautiful, too," she said. "Or she will be when she gets older." She turned suddenly to face Gina, with her mouth blood red and no chance at growing older, and wished she were anywhere but there.

Kip looked stricken also, and Thea realized how painful it must have been for him, too, to contrast Gina to healthy girls her age. Thea wished she could be sure that Gina didn't mind, but she seemed even smaller and weaker than she had been before Thea's remark.

"I don't feel so good anymore," Gina whispered.

"I know, pumpkin," Kip said, walking over to her. "Too much company. Too much excitement."

"Maybe I want to sleep," Gina said.

"Tell you what," Kip said. "Why don't we wipe off some of that lipstick, before you get it all over the pillow, and then you can take a nap." He took a couple of tissues, and gently wiped his sister's mouth. Most of the lipstick came off, and the trace that remained gave Gina the illusion of color. "Now, you take as long a nap as you want, and I'll still be here when you wake up."

"Promise?" Gina asked.

"Promise," Kip said. He kissed her again, and stroked her hair, until Gina turned over and closed her eyes.

Kip sat there for a moment, and Thea looked at them, brother and sister, sharing a connection that went deeper than any she'd ever felt with her sisters, no matter how much she loved them. If Kip could have stroked his life into Gina, Thea knew he would have. When they could hear Gina breathing deeply, Kip gestured for Thea to leave, and the two of them walked away.

"There's no reason for you to stay," Kip said, once they were in the corridor. "Gina won't be expecting you here when she wakes up."

"I know," Thea said. "I'll go in a minute." She looked at Kip, and although she tried to prevent it, a tear rolled down her cheek. "I'm sorry," she said. "I have no right."

"It's okay," Kip said, and he wiped the tear off with the same gentleness he had shown his sister. "Gina is worth some tears."

"She looks so small," Thea said. "Small and sick. I never realized."

"It was a rough weekend," Kip said. "Friday night was very bad, but then she pulled out of it. Not altogether, but she's better than she was yesterday, and she was better then than Saturday."

"Good," Thea said. "It isn't right that she should die so soon."

"It isn't going to be right whenever she dies," Kip declared. "Look, on Friday, well I didn't know. I mean, I know you'll want to be informed when . . . when she's dead, but should I call you before then?"

"You mean when she's dying?" Thea asked.

"Yeah," Kip said. "That's what I mean."

Thea had never thought about that. She'd had fantasies about Gina making a miraculous recovery, but this was the first time she really pictured the dying, the death, the funeral. "What would happen if I knew?" she asked, feeling like a coward for not agreeing on the spot.

"You could see her," Kip said. "To say good-bye. I don't know if she'll be conscious, or aware that you're there, so it would be more for you than her. If you don't want to, you certainly don't have to."

"Should I be there until it's over?" Thea asked.

Kip smiled and shook his head. "No," he said. "My mother and I will be, we've already talked about it, and maybe Dani if we can convince her to, but not you. Just family. All you'd do is come in and say good-bye, and then you can go on home."

"I can do that," Thea said. "I mean, I'd like to."

"What you mean is you can," Kip said. "Good. Now I know. When the doctors tell us, I'll tell you."

"Thank you," Thea said. "Do you think it's going to be soon?"

"No," Kip replied. "The weekend gave us a scare, and it really forced Mom and me to talk about things, but Gina should get stronger again. She might develop an infection, of course, but that risk has been there all along. The doctors think Gina might live another six months if we're lucky."

"Six months," Thea said. "That's good."

"We need the time," Kip said. "Mom does in particular. She still hasn't made peace with herself."

Thea nodded. Six months felt like forever just then. The world could change in six months. Cures could be found.

"I'd better get back in there," Kip said. "Gina's been catnapping a lot lately. If she wakes up, she'll worry about me."

"I'll go home, then," Thea said. "I'll see you Thursday."

"Wednesday," Kip said. "Remember? For dinner."

"Oh, that's right," Thea said. "Wednesday. See you then."

"And thanks, Thea," Kip said. "You said Sybil would come, and she did. Now I know I can count on you."

"Good," Thea said. "I'm glad." She smiled at Kip, and walked away from him and the hospital and a pain so intense she didn't know if she could bear to be within a hundred miles of it.

CHAPTER SEVEN

"**O**ur first dinner guest," Meg declared, as she finished setting the table. "Everything should look just right."

"It looks beautiful, Megs," Thea said. "Thank you."

"Yeah, thanks, Megs," Claire said. "This has got to be a lot better than what Kip's used to."

"I still don't see why you invited him," Sybil said. "You know Nicky doesn't want him here."

"That's why," Claire replied. "And to make Thea happy. After all, the only place she gets to see him is by a hospital bed. That's no way to conduct a courtship."

"There's no courtship to conduct," Thea declared. "And you've got to stop doing things that drive Nicky crazy. It isn't fair."

"Life isn't fair," Claire said with a shrug. "And driving Nicky crazy is one of my few real pleasures. Megs doesn't mind, do you, Megs?"

"It keeps things interesting," Meg replied. "Thea, get Nicky out from his office. I want us all to be in the living room when Kip arrives."

"Why?" Sybil asked.

"To make sure Nicky makes an appearance," Claire replied. "Shrewd thinking, Megs."

"And I don't want any teasing tonight," Meg declared. "Poor Kip will probably feel overwhelmed, anyway, and we want this to be as pleasant a dinner as possible. You owe him that, Claire, since this was all your idea."

"I'll be a saint," Claire promised.

"That'll be the day," Thea said, and she left to retrieve Nicky. He was sitting by his desk, staring out at the trees by his window. The autumn colors were starting to burst forth. "Megs wants you to join us," Thea said, hating to disturb him.

"So I won't have to make a grand entrance?" Nick asked. "Fair enough. I'll be in in a minute."

"I'll wait here for you," Thea replied, planting herself by the door.

Nicky laughed. "All right, I'm coming," he said. "I'm glad for the interruption, anyway. My thoughts weren't such pretty ones."

"What were they?" Thea asked.

"Things from the past," Nick replied. "I was thinking about my mother."

Thea was silent. She wanted Nicky to tell her more, but was afraid that anything she might say would cause him not to.

"I realized how sick she was on a day very much like

this one," Nick said. "I was sixteen, the same as you. She died a few months later."

"That must have been awful," Thea said.

Nicky shrugged and again reminded Thea of Claire. "It was a relief," he said. "My mother hated her life. She didn't will herself to be sick, but she certainly didn't try to get well."

"But she must have wanted to stay alive for you," Thea said. "She must have loved you a lot."

"Not that I ever noticed," Nick replied. "I was a constant reminder of my father."

Thea couldn't understand how that could be bad, when Nicky's father had died a hero on D-day. But maybe his stepfather had hated the comparison between himself and Nicky's father, Mr. Sebastian. Thea realized she had no names for her grandparents, and very little sense of who they were.

"Enough," Nick said. "It's ancient history. Now, what do I need to know about this Kip Claire so cavalierly invited for dinner?"

"He's very nice," Thea replied. "And he's going to go to college in New York as soon as . . . as he can."

Nicky nodded, and got up. "So Burger Bliss isn't his life's work," he said.

"It's just for the money," Thea said. "Kip's different, Nicky. He has responsibilities."

"Some people do," Nick said. They began walking toward the living room, but as they did, the doorbell rang. "You'd better get that," he said. "Before Claire does, and eats him alive."

Thea smiled, and ran to the door. She beat Claire there by half a step.

"Hi, Kip," she said, opening it to find him there.

Suddenly she felt self-conscious about all the things they had yet to do with the house. Nicky would never have permitted a real guest, someone helpful in his business dealings, to see the house in the state it was in. "Come on in."

"I brought flowers," Kip said, handing over a supermarket bouquet to her. He was wearing a suit that looked as though it had fit him better a couple of years before. Thea could see from two little nicks that he had just shaved. She realized he must have worked, visited Gina, then gone home, and changed. She wondered if his mother had insisted on the suit. She wished he weren't wearing it; he looked so gawky and ill at ease.

"You've met Claire," she said, leading him into the living room. "And Sybil. And these are my parents. Nicky, Megs, this is Kip Dozier."

"It's very nice to meet you, Kip," Meg said, giving him one of her best warm-welcoming smiles. Nicky stood still and appraised the cost of Kip's suit. "Thea's told us so much about you."

"She's been great," Kip said. "I mean, visiting Gina and all." He looked like he wanted to burst out of his suit and run. Thea wasn't sure she blamed him.

"Supper's informal tonight," Meg said. "I hope you don't mind if we eat in the kitchen. We're working on the dining room just now, and it doesn't have any furniture."

"We've been scrubbing the walls," Claire told him. "It's hell on fingernails. See." She thrust her hands at him so Kip could examine the nonexistent damage.

"Devastating," Kip said, and for the first time he sounded like himself. Thea smiled at him, and he smiled back.

"Please sit down, Kip," Meg said. "Would you like something to drink?"

"No, thank you," he said. "This is a very nice house, Mrs. Sebastian."

"It will be soon," Meg said. "Right now we're still in the scrubbing and peeling stage. I always said I wanted to renovate an old house, but now that I'm doing it, I have to question why."

"Do you want us to move?" Nick asked. "We can, Daisy, if that's what you want."

Megs laughed. "I just want the right to complain," she replied. "And then when the house is perfect, I want to be allowed to brag for two solid years."

"I hate renovating," Claire said. Thea was pleased to see she was behaving like herself, and not that strange saintlike visitor Kip had met on Monday. "I intend to complain even after the house is perfect."

"It must be difficult," Kip said. "Are you doing all the work yourself?"

"We are as a family," Meg replied.

"I supervise," Nick said. "I don't like working with my hands."

"Ah," Kip said. "I do."

"Do you, now," Nick said. "Are you good with mechanics, that sort of thing?"

"I'm good enough," Kip said. "But that isn't my primary interest."

"What is?" Meg asked.

"Sculpting," Kip replied. "I'm going to be a sculptor."

"You're kidding," Thea said. "You never told me that."

"It never came up," Kip said, and Thea realized that

was true. Their conversations almost always revolved around Gina and her needs.

"A sculptor," Nick said. "That's an interesting career choice."

"I never met anyone who wanted to be a sculptor," Claire said, as though, by age fourteen, she'd met one of everything else. "Is there any money in it?"

"Probably not," Kip replied. "And it's murder on fingernails."

"I bet," Claire said, checking hers again.

"It is an unusual ambition for a high-school student," Meg said.

"I'm no longer in high school," Kip said. "Although to be honest, I've wanted to be one for a few years now."

"But why a sculptor?" Sybil asked. "Why not a painter, or a cabinetmaker?"

Kip laughed. "Or a dentist or an accountant?" he said. "Or a sub assistant manager at a Burger Bliss?"

"We all understand why you don't want to be a sub assistant manager," Nick said. "But Sybil's question is a valid one. Why sculpting, as opposed to some other form of art?"

"Because I'm interested in immortality," Kip said. "Watercolors can be used to line bird cages. Oils can be painted over, until the only way you can find the original is by X rays. Etchings and lithographs are pleasant enough, but they don't last, either. I want my work to be around even when I'm gone."

"Have you ever sculpted Gina?" Claire asked.

Kip shook his head. "I don't do representational work," he replied. "I work in metals mostly, welding my pieces together, when I can afford it. Lately, all I've been doing is sketching things I'd like to put together someday."

"That's fascinating," Meg said. "Will art be your major when you to college?"

"Yeah," Kip said. "And burgers'll be my minor. I'm going to have to work my way through, even with the scholarship aid I'm getting."

"They must have been impressed with your work," Nick said. "To offer you the scholarship."

"I'm good," Kip said. "I'm going to get a lot better."

Thea looked at Kip and wondered where this person had come from. Where was the gentle, loving Kip who could make Gina laugh? Where was the sharp-tongued Kip who could make Thea shrivel? How many sides were there to him, and how many would she ever get to know?

"How do your parents feel about your ambitions?" Nick asked.

"My father's long gone," Kip replied. "My mother doesn't understand. It isn't that she's opposed. She simply doesn't understand."

Nicky nodded. "Sometimes it's better that way," he said. "Family can hold you back if you let them. Sometimes it's best to cut the strings and do things for yourself."

"Great," Claire said. "I'm moving out tomorrow."

"Over my dead body," Nick said. Everyone laughed, but Thea saw a flash of pain in Nicky's eyes. That was how he'd gotten out, after all. Over his mother's dead body.

The timer bell in the kitchen rang. "Dinner's ready," Meg said. "Come on everyone. Let's eat before things burn."

"Megs never burns anything," Thea said to Kip as she escorted him to the kitchen. "She's a great cook."

"I had to learn how," Meg announced as she took the casserole out of the oven and placed it on a trivet. "I didn't even know how to boil water when Nicky and I got married."

"Daisy was the original poor-little-rich-girl," Nick declared.

"Were you the original poor-little-rich-boy?" Kip asked.

Thea was relieved when Nicky laughed. "Not exactly," he said. "My family background probably wasn't all that different from yours."

"Really?" Kip said, helping himself to a biscuit.

Nicky nodded as he served himself. "My father died in the war," he said. "My mother came from a good family, but no money. When my mother remarried, I suppose it was to give me a home."

"Did it work?" Kip asked. Thea couldn't get over his nerve.

"She could have chosen better," Nick replied. "Heavy drinker, quick temper. Fast with the hands."

"I have a father like that," Kip said. "We weren't sorry to see him go."

"I was the one who left in my family," Nick said. "My mother died while I was in high school. I couldn't stay on with my stepfather. Fortunately, one of my teachers, Mr. Wilson, took me in, and later paid for my college education."

"Nicky went to Princeton," Thea said, as though that made up for all the bad things he'd had to endure.

"And a good thing, too," Nick said. "Because I met Daisy through a classmate of mine there." He smiled at her, and Thea once more had the feeling that they were the only two people in the world, and everyone else was just window dressing.

"You were lucky to have someone help you out that way," Kip declared.

"Yes, I was," Nick replied. "But once a family has achieved a certain social prominence, people are always willing to help out. It was a good thing, too, since I didn't have a specific talent to display, the way you do. I'd like to see your work sometime."

"I'd like to show it to you," Kip said, and Thea could tell that he meant it. She breathed a sigh of relief. Nicky could charm anyone, she'd always known that, but she hadn't thought he'd bother with Kip. And Kip wanted to be a sculptor. She liked that. It was more interesting than accounting and more promising than Burger Bliss.

"Daisy and Sybil are the creative ones in this family," Nick said. "Help yourself to more rice, Kip. They can do things with their hands that I marvel at."

"Thea's good, too," Meg said. "She sews very well."

"I fix things," Sybil said. "I like to take broken stuff and make it whole again."

"I wish you could do that with Gina," Kip said, smiling at her.

"I don't want to be a doctor," Sybil said. "I hate hospitals and sick people."

"Sybil!" Thea said.

"No, that's okay," Kip said. "I'm not wild about them myself."

"But you go every day," Claire said. "Thea told us."

"Sure," Kip said. "I have to. That's where Gina is."

"You'd visit daily if it were one of your sisters," Meg said. "So would you, Sybil."

Sybil scowled.

"Only if the doctors were cute," Claire said. "Maybe I should be a model. What do you think, Kip?"

"You're certainly pretty enough," Kip replied. "Are you photogenic?"

"Not that kind of model," Claire said. "An artist's model. The sort that poses in the nude and has lots of famous artists as lovers. Like the 'Naked Maja.' Would you mind that, Nicky?"

"Not as much as you would," Nick replied. "It must get cold posing in the nude. And artists are not the most sensitive of people, no insult intended, Kip. You could have as many of them as lovers as you want, Claire, but none of them will come across with emeralds and rubies."

"Then forget it," Claire said. "I'll be a courtesan instead." She smiled at Kip, who much to Thea's annoyance, smiled right back.

"Do sculptors get to have love affairs?" Sybil asked. "What if they don't have models?"

"They find someone else, then," Claire said. "They have affairs with rich men's mistresses. I saw that on a miniseries once. She was a poor girl from the slums, only she was beautiful, of course, and this rich mobster discovered her working as a coatcheck girl and she became his mistress and then he got shot, and some other rich guy, but respectable, rescued her, only he wouldn't marry her because he had this fiancée from the right side of the tracks, and she met this artist, I think he was a sculptor, and he made beautiful statues of her, and he sold them to a gallery, and the rich guy's fiancée bought one for him as a wedding present, because she didn't know he was really in love with her, and then the rich guy got his present, and he didn't know what to do, because it was his girlfriend, only his fiancée didn't know that, and the sculptor used the money he got for selling the statue to go to Europe, and he tried to convince the girlfriend to go with him, only she wouldn't. And then the fiancée met the girlfriend at the gallery, and she brought her home to meet the rich guy. That was the best scene. They tried to pretend she didn't have any clothes on when she modeled, but you could tell they faked it."

"My sister Dani saw that miniseries, too," Kip declared. "That was when she decided it would be okay for me to be a sculptor."

"Maybe we should get rid of the TV," Nick said to Megs. "If that's the sort of thing our daughters are watching on it."

"Only Claire, Nicky," Thea said. "I never watch TV, and Sybil only watches educational stuff."

"I like trash," Claire said. "I intend to lead a wonderfully trashy life as soon as possible."

"What happened when the rich guy met his girlfriend?" Sybil asked.

"I don't know," Claire said. "That was all on part one of the miniseries, and I never got to see part two."

"Ask Dani," Kip said. "She committed the whole thing to memory."

"Of course she did," Claire said. "It was research for her. I'd memorize a miniseries, too, if it told me all about what Evvie was going to be doing the rest of her life."

Kip laughed. "I don't think that miniseries was exactly my life story," he said. "From what Dani told me, there was no welding."

"I'd like to weld," Sybil said. "Would you teach me sometime, Kip? Not so I could sculpt. Just so I could weld."

"If it's all right with your parents," Kip replied. "Welding can be dangerous."

"I'll be careful," Sybil said. "May I, Nicky?"

"We'll talk about it," Nick replied. "Thea, would you

please pass me the string beans. Daisy, this is truly delicious."

"Thank you," Meg said. "Do you like to cook, Kip, or does Burger Bliss knock all that out of you?"

"It certainly helps," Kip said, and soon they were all talking about fast food and what Kip's job entailed.

After supper, they went back to the living room, and continued to talk. Thea couldn't get over how well Kip fit in, and how easily he and Nicky conversed. By the end of the evening, even Kip's suit seemed to fit him better.

"I'd better get going," he said around nine. "Mrs. Sebastian, dinner was delicious. Thank you for having me."

"I'm glad you came," Meg said. "Do come again, Kip."

"I'd like to," Kip said.

"I'll walk you to the door," Thea said. She got up, and went with Kip. They walked outside, and stood together in the cool night air.

"I like your family," Kip told her. "I have to admit, I didn't expect to."

"We're never what people expect," Thea replied. "We always surprise people. That's what Sam says. He's Evvie's boyfriend. He said none of us were the way he pictured." She realized she was babbling, and wished she could figure out a way to stop.

"Your father," Kip began. "Well, I just assumed he'd be some fat cat, you know, born to the money. And then when you told me you didn't always have money, I figured he'd be a bum, maybe like my father only with more money to burn. I didn't expect someone who was so much like me."

"He was thinking about his mother earlier," Thea

said. "He told me. He doesn't usually talk about his family. I guess the memories are too painful."

"I won't talk about mine, either," Kip said. "When I'm gone, they'll be gone, too."

Thea shook her head. "Family isn't like that," she said. "They're part of you. You always carry them with you."

"Only if you like them," Kip said.

Do you like me? Thea wanted to ask. Will you carry me with you?

Kip looked down at Thea. She waited for him to kiss her. But instead he said, "I'd better get going. Will you be visiting Gina, tomorrow?"

"Of course," Thea replied. "My regular Thursday visit."

Kip nodded. "See you then," he said. "And thanks again."

"You're welcome," Thea said. She watched as Kip walked away, and wondered whether his not kissing her had meant more than a kiss would have.

CHAPTER EIGHT

"**I**'d better get going," Thea said to Gina. "I promised Megs I'd help her with supper tonight, and I have that big math test to study for."

Gina nodded. "Will you come again on Thursday?" she asked.

"Of course I will," Thea replied. She bent over and kissed Gina on the forehead. "Now you do what the doctors tell you, and get some more sleep," she said. "See you Thursday."

"I'll try," Gina said.

"I'll walk you out," Kip declared. "I'll be back in a minute, Gina. And if you fall asleep, I'll wait until you wake up."

Gina smiled at her brother. Thea thought she'd start crying. She could see how much weaker Gina had gotten in the past few weeks, and the toll it was taking on Kip as well.

"Thanks for coming," Kip said to her once they were in the corridor. "I know it's tough on you."

"It's tougher on you," Thea replied. "How are you doing?"

"I'm okay," Kip said, but then he scowled. "No I'm not," he said. "It sucks. I hope you never have to watch someone you love die."

I am now, Thea thought, but decided it would be presumptuous to say so. She couldn't be feeling a tenth of what Kip was. "How's your mother taking it?" she asked instead. Not that Kip's mother was safe territory.

"It's getting to her, too," Kip said. "I hardly see Dani anymore. God only knows where she's spending her nights."

"Does she see Gina?" Thea asked.

Kip shook his head. "Part of me wants to force her to come, for her sake more than Gina's. But most of me just doesn't care. I won't be around when Dani starts feeling guilty. She can deal with it then, all by herself."

Thea wished she could reach out and comfort Kip, but there was nothing she could say that he wanted to hear. She kept walking down the hallway, and tried not to look at him. "Do the doctors think Gina'll get any stronger?" she asked, trying to sound casual.

"The doctors are jerks," Kip declared. "They insist on talking to Mom, who only takes in half of what they say, and she tells me half of that and then I'm supposed to explain it to her. As far as I can see, they're worried about Gina picking up another serious infection. She has no resistance at this point. If she doesn't get sick, then I don't know, maybe another three months, maybe more.

If she does, it'll be a matter of days. I'd really like her to be alive for Christmas. Dammit, is that asking too much? One more Christmas. I have money this year, I've been saving, and I'd like to give her something, the perfect Christmas present. Gina's entitled. She's never had anything her entire damned life except sickness and pain, and just for once I'd like to see her eyes light up, I want to see her happy about something. I don't even know what to get her, but it'll be perfect. I don't care what it costs. I'd rather spend the money on that one perfect present than on the biggest damn funeral in town."

"Oh, Kip," Thea said.

"What?" Kip said. "I said the *f* word? Funeral? We're going to have to have one, you know. It's a lot more in Gina's future than some stupid Christmas present that's supposed to make up for her whole stupid life."

"Do you want me to go shopping with you?" Thea asked.

"For what?" Kip replied. "Coffins?"

Thea rubbed her forehead. "For Christmas presents," she said. "I'd like to get Gina something, too."

"Sure," Kip said. "If she's around in December, we'll go shopping together."

"She will be," Thea promised. "This may sound dumb, but I just can't see a kid dying right before Christmas."

"You're right," Kip said. "It does sound dumb."

Thea resisted an impulse to kick him. Instead she began walking faster and moved a couple of steps away from him.

"I'm sorry," Kip said, grabbing her arm to slow her down. "I am, Thea. It'll be good to go shopping with you. You'll have a much better idea of what to get than I would. And I appreciate all you've done for Gina. Your visits are just about the only thing she has to look forward to, and you've never let her down. I know it can't be easy on you, either, and I've been taking you for granted. Actually that's a compliment, but you might not see it that way. Thank you."

"You're welcome," Thea replied. She yearned to take Kip in her arms, hold him, comfort him. Instead she smiled. "Gina'll get better," she said. "I don't mean she'll get well, but she'll get stronger. And you'll give her the most beautiful Christmas present ever."

Kip nodded. "I'll get you something, too," he said. "Gina and I will figure out just the right present for you, and it'll be from both of us. Gina'll like that."

"I'll like it, too," Thea said. "Kip, you know you can call me if you need me."

"I know," he said. "And I'm grateful."

"All right," Thea said. "Well, I'd better get going. I have a lot of homework to do. That math test scares me."

"You'll ace it," Kip said. "See you on Thursday."

"Thursday," Thea said. She opened the door and walked out into the crisp October day. She didn't know how much more she could take. Each visit with Gina was a small agony, and seeing Kip in so much pain only made things worse. She knew she should feel enriched by being a Friendly Visitor, grateful for the spiritual lessons that befriending Gina had taught her. But for one awful glorious moment, Thea hated everything about the Friendly Visitors, and wished that all those who'd involved her in the program would have to endure half of what she'd been through in the past month.

She walked down the hill toward her house, and was shocked to find Sybil half a block ahead of her. "Sybil?" she called. "What are you doing here?"

"Oh, hi, Thea," Sybil said. "I'm collecting candy wrappers."

"Of course," Thea said. "How could I not have known."

Sybil stuck her tongue out at her. It was such a wonderful healthy twelve-year-old thing to do that Thea almost hugged her. "It's for my refund offer," Sybil explained. "I got the form from the supermarket bulletin board. If you collect one hundred candy wrappers from the right brands, they'll send you twenty bucks."

"You're kidding," Thea said. "Twenty dollars?"

Sybil nodded. "They expect you to buy all the candy," she said. "And save the wrappers and mail them back in. Only instead of buying the candy, I've been looking for wrappers on the sidewalks. I love litter. I've been taking walks for a week now, and I'm already up to nineteen wrappers, and I have until December first to find the other eighty-one."

"Are you going to use the twenty for Christmas presents?" Thea asked.

"Are you crazy?" Sybil said. "I'm saving it."

"For what?" Thea asked.

"For emergencies," Sybil said. "So the next time Nicky goes belly-up, I'll have some cash reserves. I'm not going to waste good money on stupid Christmas presents."

"First of all, Nicky isn't going to go belly-up," Thea said. "We're in great shape from Harrison, and he has two good deals going here already. And secondly, there's nothing stupid about Christmas presents. I always get you something nice, and so does Evvie, and so do Nicky and Megs. You're old enough to start giving us nice things back."

"Nicky's getting Megs a piano," Sybil replied. "And

Megs'll get Nicky something expensive, too, a yacht maybe, or some fancy watch. They always give each other great stuff when Nicky's in the money, so they don't need anything from me. Evvie has Sam to give her things, and Sam has money, so it'll be something nice, too. The stuff Claire wants, I can't afford, so there's no point worrying about her."

"That leaves me," Thea pointed out.

"I'll get you something," Sybil said. Her eyes lit up and the next thing Thea knew, she was running down the street yelling, "Hey, mister!"

Thea followed Sybil, not knowing what had excited her so. Maybe Sybil had witnessed a bank robbery, and would get a reward for stopping the thief. That should give her a healthy cash reserve.

"Don't throw out that candy wrapper!" Sybil cried, and Thea considered dying on the spot.

"I was going to put it in the trash can," the man protested. "See." He pointed to the can, and made an elaborate gesture of disposing of the wrapper properly.

"I need that wrapper," Sybil said. "It's an Mmm Mmm bar. That'll be number twenty."

"Number twenty what?" the man asked.

"For my refund offer," Sybil said. "Now all I'll need is eighty more and I can earn twenty dollars. Assuming you'll give it to me. If you don't, I'll take it out of the trash can, but I'd really rather you just handed it over. Do you mind?"

"I can live with it," the man said, and handed the wrapper to Sybil. "Didn't your mother teach you not to take candy from strangers."

"It isn't candy," Sybil said. "It's a candy wrapper. Thank you."

"You're welcome," the man said. "Are both of you collecting wrappers?" He looked pointedly at Thea, who turned bright red.

"Only my sister," Thea said. "She's a collector."

"Every family needs one," the man said. "My name is Peter Grass. "I'm a reporter for the *Sentinel*."

"We get the *Sentinel*," Sybil told him. "It's a good paper."

"Thank you," Mr. Grass said. "You know, if you need the extra money, they're always looking for paperboys. Or girls."

"We don't need the money," Thea said quickly. "Do we, Sybil?"

"No, we're rich," Sybil said. "I just like doing refunding because it's like getting something for nothing."

"That's how the rich get richer," Mr. Grass declared. "Do many of your friends refund also, Sybil?"

"We don't have any clubs, if that's what you mean," Sybil said. "I know one kid who collects bottles for the refunds on them, but I don't think that's fair."

"Why not?" Mr. Grass asked. Thea sighed. She wasn't sure if it was safe to leave Sybil in the arms of the press, but on the other hand, she really wanted to get home before Sybil had a chance to philosophize.

"Because poor people collect bottles," Sybil said, not giving Thea the time to decide on a course of action. "And they really need the money. I figure I'm not hurting anybody by collecting candy wrappers, because most people just drop them on the sidewalks like litter. Not that you were going to. But poor people don't know about the refund offer, and they probably wouldn't have a place to keep the wrappers until they get the whole hundred. That's a lot of candy wrappers to carry if you're homeless. But bottles, they can just collect that day and turn in at night, so it's quick money for them. It must be awful being homeless. What do you think?"

"I think that's an interesting attitude," Mr. Grass said. "What's your full name, Sybil?"

"Sybil Ward Sebastian," Sybil replied. "Ward's a family name, like Julia Ward Howe. My mother's from Boston."

"Have you been living in Briarton long?" Mr. Grass asked.

"Just a couple of months," Sybil said. "But I really like it. Only it's too clean. Not enough people litter, and a lot of times when they do, they leave the wrong kind of candy wrappers. I'm collecting Mmm Mmms, and Mmm Mmms with Almonds, and Wattabars, and Sweet Somethings, and Yummie Juniors. I have twenty and only one of them is a Yummie Junior. Have you ever had one? They really stink."

"I don't think Mr. Grass is interested anymore," Thea said, hoping that was true. "We'd better get home now."

"Sybil Ward Sebastian," Mr. Grass said. "It's been a pleasure meeting you."

"Thank you," Sybil said. "Hey, I have an idea. Do the other reporters eat candy bars? I could go to your office and collect the wrappers if they do."

"Sybil!" Thea screeched. "You'll have to excuse her," she said. "She's a straight-A student in obsessive-compulsiveness."

Mr. Grass laughed. "Just one more thing," he said. "What are you going to do with the money, once you get your hundred wrappers?"

"I'm going to use it for the poor," Sybil replied.

"We really have to be going," Thea said. She grabbed

Sybil and pulled her away before she started ransacking the garbage can. When they were a safe distance from Mr. Grass, Thea turned to Sybil and said, "Use it for the poor?"

"Sure," Sybil said. "Me. When Nicky flops next time, I'll be poor."

"You're worse than Claire," Thea said.

"I just believe in being prepared," Sybil replied. "I'm going to stay out and collect more wrappers. I want to have thirty by Friday."

"Be my guest," Thea said. She walked home marveling at Sybil's nerve. If Sybil was after a hundred wrappers, she'd be sure to get them, probably before nightfall.

Thea walked in through the back door and found her parents kissing in front of the sink. They didn't seem to notice that she'd come in, so she walked back to the door and slammed it loudly. They broke their embrace, but Nicky traced Megs's face with his fingers, and Megs continued to stare into Nicky's eyes.

"I'm home," Thea said.

"So we heard," Nick said. "How was your day?"

"Hard," Thea replied. She went to the refrigerator and got an apple. Gina is dying, she wanted to say, and I never know what to say to Kip, and Sybil just made a fool of herself in public. But Nicky didn't want to hear any of those things, so she bit into the apple instead.

"I had a great day," Nick said. "The bank is very interested in financing the factory-conversion project, if I can swing just one more investor, and Ed Chambers has all but agreed to the plan."

"That's great, Nicky," Thea said, taking another bite. Ordinarily, she loved hearing about Nicky's schemes, but ordinarily she didn't spend an hour watching a little girl die.

"I've been thinking," Nick said, and he took Megs's hand and entwined his fingers with hers. "About Thanksgiving. What is it, a month away?"

"Give or take," Meg said, smiling at him.

"Why not have a really big Thanksgiving this year," Nick said. "It seems to me we have more than enough to be thankful about. Briarton's already a big success, and Evvie's doing well at college, and this house is turning into a showcase, thanks to you, and I feel like telling the world how happy I am. What do you think?"

Megs beamed. "A really big Thanksgiving dinner?" she asked. "Who could we invite?"

"Let's tell Evvie to bring Sam here," Nick said. "She'll like that. And we could invite Clark, too. He can have Thea's room, and Thea and Evvie can move in with Claire and Sybil. Sam can sleep on the sofa bed in my office."

"Do you really want Clark?" Meg asked.

"Sure," Nick said. "It'd be good for him to see me prosperous. He'll worry about you less."

"Could we invite Aunt Grace also?" Meg asked. "If we're going to do a true family Thanksgiving, we ought to invite her, too."

Nick grimaced, but then he grinned. "Why not," he said. "It'll be a cold day in hell before she's willing to come. Let's invite her just to drive her crazy."

"What if she agrees?" Meg asked. "She just might call your bluff."

"Then we'll roll out the red carpet," Nick replied. "That's the appropriate color for Sam, too. If Aunt Grace actually deigns to enter my home, I'll treat her like royalty. I'll do better. I'll treat her almost as well as she expects to be treated."

"It sounds wonderful," Meg declared. "I'd love to have Clark come. And I've been so afraid Evvie would decide to spend Thanksgiving with Sam's family instead of coming home."

"This Thanksgiving we'll have her here," Nick promised. "Maybe we could make a tradition out of this. Open our family up a little bit. I've been selfish, wanting to keep you all close to me, not letting anyone else in. But there's no point, not with the girls growing up. They have worlds of their own now. Don't you, Thea?"

Thea nodded. She hadn't been sure her parents remembered she was in the room with them. Now that they'd reassured her, she took another bite of apple.

"How is Gina, dear?" Meg asked.

Thea swallowed. "Bad," she said. "Kip is hoping she makes it until Christmas."

"That poor kid," Nick said. "Both of them."

"I wish there was something more we could do for them," Meg said. "For you, too, Thea. I know how hard it's been for you, becoming attached to a girl who's so ill."

"It's okay," Thea said. She realized she sounded like Kip. What was there about death that made you so defensive? "Kip's the one who's really suffering."

"Let's invite him for Thanksgiving also," Nick said. "What do you think, Daisy?"

"I think that's a lovely idea," Meg replied. "Do you think Kip would come?"

"I don't know," Thea said. "He does have a family."

"I would have loved it if someone had invited me for Thanksgiving dinner," Nick said. "After my mother died."

"Didn't you have Thanksgiving dinner with Mr. Wilson?" Thea asked. "I thought you moved in with him right after."

"Freshman year at Princeton," Nick said. "I'd never felt so alone. Mr. Wilson had died by then also, and all the other guys had families to go home to, and none of them knew me well enough to extend an invitation. I don't know if I would have accepted, anyway. Thanksgiving that year, and Christmas. There were maybe a half dozen of us in the house, less than that at Christmas. There was a big dinner, of course, so we wouldn't mind what we were missing, but that only made things worse. It forced me to face what everyone else had, a loving family, a place to go home to."

"By sophomore year, things were different," Meg said.

"Oh, yeah," Nick said. "By sophomore year, I had you, and holidays were spent freezing outside your bedroom window, tossing stones against the glass to catch a glimpse of you without Grace knowing it."

Megs smiled. "You wanted us to elope that Christmas," she said. "I never thought I'd be able to talk you out of it."

"I was afraid I'd lose you, otherwise," Nick said.

"You would have lost everything else if we'd done it," Meg said. "And you should have known you would never lose me."

"I still don't know it," Nick said. "Every day with you is an astonishment."

"Let's invite Kip," Meg said. "And his mother and sister. Is that all right with you, Nicky?"

"It's fine with me," Nick said. "Thea, would that make things all right for Kip?"

"I don't know," Thea said, trying not to keel over from the shock. "I can ask him."

"And maybe the hospital will let Gina join us," Meg said. "Just for an hour or two. If I were her mother, it would make me so happy to see my daughter out of the hospital, surrounded by family and friends, if only for an hour."

"Let's do it," Nick said. "Thea, do you want to invite Kip's family, or would you rather we did it directly?"

"I'll do it," Thea said. "Maybe on Thursday, when I see him at the hospital."

"Great," Nick said. "This is going to be a perfect Thanksgiving, the kind I used to dream of. A Thanksgiving where we have so much prosperity and love that there's enough left over to share with others."

CHAPTER NINE

"Well look at this," Nick said, as he finished his last sip of coffee.

"What?" Meg asked.

"This column in the *Sentinel*," Nick said. "It's all about Sybil."

"Oh, no." Thea groaned, but her parents didn't seem to hear her. Instead, they both bent over the newspaper and read Peter Grass's column.

"This is great," Nick said, and much to Thea's surprise, he sounded as though he meant it. "Sybil's already left, hasn't she?"

"Five minutes ago," Meg replied. "Thea, Claire, you should be leaving now, too."

"I want to see the column," Claire said, and she joined her parents at the table. "Thea, this is all about Sybil."

"So I've heard," Thea said. "I was there when she met Mr. Grass. Does he make her sound like a total idiot?"

"More like a Nobel Prize winner," Claire replied. "In one sentence, he uses *ingenuity, dedication,* and *self-sacrifice.*"

"You're kidding," Thea said, but she skimmed the column and discovered Claire was accurate. According to Mr. Grass, Sybil was a cross between Rachel Carson and Mother Teresa.

"I have to buy a copy for Aunt Grace," Meg said. "And one for Clark as well. They'll get such a kick out of it."

"We'll need one for Evvie, also," Nick said. "I suppose you two would each like one of your own."

"I couldn't live without it," Claire said.

"I could," Thea said, but she was ignored. Instead, Claire led her outside, and they began walking to the high school.

"She's such a hypocrite," Thea complained. "She told that reporter she was earning the money for the poor, and she meant herself. How can she get away with that kind of thing?"

"Sybil gets away with everything," Claire replied. "You've never noticed that?"

"No," Thea said. "I thought you were the one who got away with things."

Claire laughed. "I'm the one who tries to," she said. "Sybil isn't as obvious about it, but she's a lot more successful. Evvie and Sybil. When they sneeze, Nicky thinks it's a major accomplishment."

Thea thought about it for a moment. "We're all proud of Evvie," she said. "Evvie does things to make you proud of her."

"Evvie does it without really trying, though," Claire said. "She gets great grades, but you never see her cramming. She makes friends easily, guys fall in love with her even though she isn't beautiful, like I am. Even you're prettier than she is, but guys don't fall in love with you. There's just something about Evvie. I think it's because she's firstborn. It gives you an aura."

"Someday someone will fall in love with me," Thea said. "Am I really prettier than Evvie?"

"Sure," Claire said. "You're very pretty in a kind of wishy-washy, uninteresting way. Like Megs. So's Evvie, but you do a better job with it."

"I still don't get it," Thea said. "If Peter Grass had written a column about you or me, Nicky would have been hysterical. The only kind of publicity he likes is the kind he dictates. But someone writes an entire column about how Sybil goes begging for candy wrappers on the street, and Nicky starts making lists of people to show off to."

"Sybil's his favorite," Claire said.

"Nicky doesn't have favorites," Thea replied automatically.

"Boy, are you blind," Claire said. "Of course Nicky has favorites. So does Megs. She's always liked Evvie best, and Nicky likes Sybil. That doesn't mean they don't love you, or even me. It just means they let them get away with more."

Thea decided she wasn't comfortable with the idea of her parents having favorites. Besides, it was exactly the sort of thing Claire would accuse them of because she was feeling left out. And if Claire felt left out, that was because she never made any effort to cooperate. "You're the one who's blind," she declared, and she walked ahead to prevent Claire from continuing the conversation. She could hear Claire's laughter follow her down the street, but that was a sound Thea was used to ignoring. Claire was always laughing at her, or at Nicky, or at the things they held most dear. She could laugh her head off, as far as Thea was concerned. Claire would never understand how much Nicky and Megs loved their daughters, and how equal that love was. Even if it was true that Sybil got away with all kinds of things Thea knew would be a disaster for her to attempt.

Fortunately, no one at school had read the column, or if they had, they didn't connect Sybil's name with Thea's. Thea made it through the school day without having to talk about it, which was fine with her. She dreaded the thought that people would start handing her their candy wrappers to give to Sybil for her collection for the poor. Thea was accustomed to being Evvie Sebastian's sister, because everyone liked Evvie, and being Claire Sebastian's sister, because Claire was, unfortunately, as beautiful as she thought she was, but she wasn't ready to become Saint Sybil Sebastian's sister as well.

She found herself thinking of Gina all afternoon, and decided to go to the hospital after school, even though it was a Wednesday and she'd be a day off schedule. She might not stay long, but she needed right then to see someone who cared about her, and Gina certainly fit that description.

Thea went to the hospital as soon as the last bell rang. She didn't know what to expect. Somehow she thought the hospital might only exist on Mondays and Thursdays, or Gina might be unconscious except during those hours when Thea visited. Part of her was nervous about going on a Wednesday, as though that violated a religion. Would the nurses let her in? Would Kip be angry?

But the nurses didn't seem to care, and Kip wasn't around when Thea walked in. Gina was lying on her bed, looking better than she had on Monday.

"Thea!" she said. "Look at the flowers. Look at the teddy bear."

Thea looked. There was a small bouquet of sweetheart roses by Gina's bed, and a midsized huggable bear resting on her pillow.

"They're wonderful," Thea said, sitting down on the bed by Gina's side. "Where did they come from?"

"Your parents," Gina replied. "They came to visit me this morning. Both of them. Your father brought me the flowers and your mother gave me the teddy bear."

"You're kidding," Thea said. "Did they say why they came?"

"Just to meet me," Gina said. "They said you told them so much about me, and they'd met Kip, so they wanted to meet me, too. Your father is so handsome. I never saw such a handsome man except on TV. Why isn't he a star?"

"Because he never wanted to be one," Thea replied. She wasn't sure how many more shocks she could take that day.

"And your mother looks like an angel," Gina continued. "I think when I go to heaven that's what all the angels are going to look like."

"Heaven?" Thea said. "What makes you think you're going to heaven?"

"Why should I go to hell?" Gina asked. "I've never done anything bad. I've never had the chance."

"No," Thea said. "That's not what I mean. Of course

you aren't going to go to hell. I mean, why are you thinking about going to heaven?"

"That's where dead people go," Gina declared. "Mom says so. She says in heaven I'll never be sick and lots of people there will love me. My grandparents are already in heaven, so they're waiting for me. I hope they'll recognize me, because I haven't seen them in a long time. And I had a dog when I was real little, and a car hit him, so he's in heaven waiting for me, too. It used to scare me that I'd go to heaven and no one I knew would be dead yet, except maybe my father. We don't know where he is, but he wouldn't be in heaven, anyway. Mom made a list of all the people in heaven who are waiting for me. My grandparents, and my dog, and my uncle Harvey. I never met him, but Mom says he'll know me. I guess my grandparents will introduce us. And there'll be angels there, and they'll all look blond and beautiful like your mother."

Thea wished with all her might that she'd had the sense not to visit on a Wednesday. Wednesday was clearly Gina's day to deal with death, and Thea had no desire to deal with Gina's dealings.

"Let's talk about something else," she said. "What a great bear. I used to have one just like it. Do you have a name for it?"

Gina shook her head. "What did you name yours?" she asked.

Thea knew the bear had had a name, but she could no longer remember it. "Montague," she said. They were studying *Romeo and Juliet* in English, and Montague was the first name she could think of. At least it was better for a bear than Romeo.

"I don't think I want to call mine Montague," Gina

said. "Your mother said she knew I was probably a little too sophisticated for a teddy bear, but she thought it might get lonely sometimes here, and there's nothing better when you're lonely than to have a teddy bear. And your father said he brought me pink roses because that's the flower he always gave his daughters on their twelfth birthdays. Did he give you pink roses then?"

Thea nodded. Just then she had no idea what kind of flowers, if any, Nicky had given her, but pink roses sounded like him. "It isn't your birthday, is it?" she asked.

"No," Gina replied. "My mom came in while they were here, and your parents talked to her, and I could see they made her smile. Mom doesn't smile a lot. Kip does, but he doesn't always mean it. He just smiles to make me feel better. And they brought me the newspaper with the article about Sybil. I was so proud. I know her, and she has an article all about how nice she is. I just wish Mr. Grass had called me. I would have told him about how Sybil came to the hospital just to visit me and he could have put that in the paper. I'm keeping the article. Your parents said I could. They said they bought lots of copies to give to everybody, and they wanted me to have one. My mom doesn't buy the newspaper, but she said she was going to go out and get a copy, too, because she feels like she knows Sybil already because I've told her so much about her. You're so lucky to have such beautiful parents."

"Yes, I know," Thea said.

"I can't wait to go to heaven if everyone's going to be that nice," Gina said. "Do you think they have teddy bears in heaven?"

"Sure," Thea said. Why not? "Lots of teddy bears and roses and beautiful angels."

Gina nodded. "Mom says if I'm real good once I get to heaven I can become an angel, too. I'd like to be an angel. Then I'd look just like your mother."

"You look pretty beautiful to me right now," Thea said.

"I'll look even better when I'm an angel," Gina replied. "When I'm dead and in heaven, I'll be the most beautiful angel there."

"What's this about heaven?" Kip asked. Thea wished he weren't so light on his feet. His arrivals always startled her.

"When I'm dead," Gina said. "I'll be an angel, and then I'll look just like Thea's mother. Hi, Kip."

"Hi, pumpkin," Kip said. He bent over and kissed Gina. "Uh, Thea, could I talk to you for a moment."

"Sure," Thea said, delighted to get away from Gina's discussions of heaven. She followed Kip out of the room into the corridor.

"What kind of garbage are you feeding her?" Kip asked once they were alone.

"Garbage?" Thea said.

"Heaven and angels who look like your mother," Kip said. "Why in God's name are you talking about dying to Gina?"

"I'm not," Thea said. "She brought it up. I never told her anything about heaven, except that there are teddy bears there, and that's because she just asked me. Your mother's the one who's been telling her about heaven."

"I'll kill her," Kip said. "I swear, I'll kill her."

"Why?" Thea said. "She has to tell Gina something."

"No, she doesn't," Kip declared. "If Gina wants to

know, she can ask me. Mom doesn't have to fill her head with fairy tales."

"Maybe it isn't a fairy tale to your mother," Thea said. "Maybe she needs to believe that Gina's going to go to a wonderful heaven where her grandparents will look out for her and she'll become a beautiful angel. It might not hurt you to believe it, either."

"Do you?" Kip asked. "Is that what you believe?"

"It doesn't matter what I believe," Thea said. "What matters is that Gina knows she's going to die, and she's made peace with it by picturing herself in some perfect heaven. If she wants the angels to look like my mother, then fine, they look like my mother. Would you rather she went around singing 'The worms crawl in'?"

Kip rubbed his eyes, and Thea had some sense of just how tired he was. "I'm sorry," he said. "I don't want her to die."

"I know," Thea said. "Kip, you're exhausted. Why don't you take the day off? I'll stay with Gina and we can talk some more about heaven, and you go for a walk or get some sleep while nobody's home or make some sketches for sculptures you want to do. Gina won't mind. She's had an exciting day, anyway. My parents came to visit. I'll stay until her suppertime, I promise."

"Would you mind?" Kip asked.

"I wouldn't volunteer if I minded," Thea said, uncomfortably aware that that was not always the case. "Let's go back, and you can say good-bye to Gina."

"Thank you," Kip said. "What are you doing here anyway on a Wednesday?"

"I wanted to be someplace where I was needed," Thea said.

"You picked the right spot," Kip said. He stared at

Thea, and once again she had the sensation of a kiss not given. "Sometimes I think of how much we owe you, and then I can't even think about it, so I stop."

"That's okay," Thea said. "I don't know if this is the right moment, but my parents want your whole family to join us for Thanksgiving dinner "

"What do you mean by whole family?" Kip asked warily.

"Your mother and Dani and you," Thea said. "Gina also, if the doctors will let her."

"Why?" Kip asked.

"I'm not really sure myself," Thea admitted. "Holidays have always been just for family, but I guess they figure things are different now that Evvie's in college. She wanted to spend Thanksgiving with Sam last year, and Nicky and Megs wouldn't let her, so maybe they figure if they invite Sam to our house, that'll solve that problem. And then if they're inviting Sam, they might as well invite other people like Clark."

"Who's Clark?" Kip asked.

"He's the guy everyone thought Megs would marry," Thea said. "Think of him as an honorary uncle."

Kip laughed. "My mother's brought home plenty of uncles," he said. "We didn't think to call them honorary, though."

"It isn't the same thing," Thea said. "Anyway, if they're going to have Sam and Clark, then I guess they felt the whole world was open to them to invite, and they decided on you next. Only they couldn't just ask you without asking your mother and sisters, too, so that's why you've all been invited."

"I don't know," Kip said. "Mom doesn't handle holidays too well. And Dani's likely to throw herself at this Clark guy, if not at your father."

"We'd really like you all to come," Thea said. "Please, Kip. It's important."

"Why?" Kip asked. "From what I could see, your family is pretty self-sufficient."

"We always have been," Thea replied. "That's why it matters that you come. It's like Nicky's finally realizing there are other people on the planet. They're really making an effort. Inviting you, and coming to see Gina today. Please say you'll come for Thanksgiving."

Kip smiled. "If it's that important, then of course we'll come," he said. "After all you've done for Gina, the least we can do is eat turkey together."

"Fine," Thea said. "Come on, now. Let's get back to Gina before she thinks we've eloped." She blushed as soon as she said it.

"She wants us to," Kip said as they walked back into the ward. "She keeps telling me to ask you out on a date."

Thea tried to laugh. It came out a cackle.

"Yeah," Kip said. "That's what I do. Laugh."

Why? Thea wanted to ask, but since she was the one sort of laughing, she decided not to pursue it. There was probably a perfectly good reason why Kip thought it was funny that he should ask her out, but Thea was in no mood to learn what that reason was.

"Good," Kip said. "She's still awake."

"Just barely, it looks like," Thea said.

"Hi there, pumpkinhead," Kip whispered to his sister.

"Are you going to stay, too?" Gina asked.

Thea could see Kip wavering. "No," she said. "Kip

has to go home and do some things. I'll stay with you instead."

"Is that okay, pumpkin?" Kip asked. "If you want, I'll stay instead."

"If you go away, will I see you again?" Gina asked.

"Tomorrow," Kip said. "I promise."

"What if I die?" Gina asked.

"Gina, you're not going to die," Kip said.

"Maybe I will," she said, "if you're not here, and then I'll never see you again."

"Gina!" Thea said sharply. "Let your brother go home for a few hours. It's not that big a deal. He'll see you tomorrow."

"No, it's okay," Kip said. "It was a dumb idea. I'll stay here with you, pumpkin, just like I always do."

"Good," Gina said, and she snuggled next to her brother. "This is my new teddy bear. His name is Dirk and I'm going to take him to heaven with me."

"That's good," Kip murmured, and Thea watched helplessly as he cradled his sister in his weary arms.

CHAPTER TEN

Thea woke up early Thanksgiving morning and felt herself surrounded by love. She and Evvie were crowded into Sybil's bed, while Sybil and Claire were sharing Claire's. Thea's bedroom was occupied by Sam and Scotty Hughes, whom Clark had brought along for the weekend. Clark was in Nicky's office, and Nicky and Megs were probably already starting the feast. In a few hours, Kip and his whole family would be joining them. Everyone would be there, except for Aunt Grace, who, as Nick had predicted, had refused to attend. Which was fine with all of them.

"Wake up," Thea whispered to Evvie, and gave her a gentle kick to emphasize the point.

"Wha?" Evvie muttered.

"Wake up," Thea said. "Let's get going."

"Go away," Evvie said.

Thea laughed to herself, and then realized she could live without the competition for the bathroom. So she used it while she had the chance, then went downstairs to see how things were going.

Not only were her parents up and about, but so were Sam and Scotty. Thea was glad of the chance to check Scotty out. She didn't know much about him, except that he was seventeen, went to some posh prep school, was a distant cousin of Clark's, and the younger brother of Schyler Hughes, the boy Evvie hadn't fallen in love with the summer she spent at Aunt Grace's. Now that Thea thought about it, that was a lot to know about a stranger.

"Did you sleep well, dear?" Meg asked, giving Thea a good morning kiss.

"Fine," Thea lied. Actually she and her sisters had stayed up half the night talking and giggling.

"Evvie's still asleep?" Sam asked.

Thea smiled at Sam. This wasn't his first visit to the Sebastians', but he still didn't seem at ease, not without Evvie by his side. "She'll be up real soon," Thea promised. "I kicked her a few times to rouse her."

"Thank you," Sam said.

"Did you sleep well, Scotty?" Thea asked, pouring herself some orange juice.

"Yes, thank you," Scotty replied. He was handsome, Thea noticed, with light brown hair and hazel eyes. "It's very nice of your family to take me in for Thanksgiving."

"When Clark explained the situation, we were only too happy to," Meg said. "Scotty's parents are in Syria, and his brother Schyler is spending the weekend in Paris. Isn't that right, Scotty?"

Scotty nodded.

"Paris," Sam said. "That sounds about right for Schyler."

"I'd rather be here," Scotty said. "I really liked Evvie that summer we spent at Eastgate. And Clark's told me so much about the rest of you, that it's a pleasure to finally meet you."

"How are we shaping up?" Thea asked. "Compared to what Clark's told you."

"You're much prettier than I thought you'd be," Scotty said. "Everyone else is pretty much as described."

Thea blushed. Sam laughed. "Schyler was better with compliments than anybody I've ever met," he declared. "I guess it runs in the family."

"But I'm sincere," Scotty said. "That's how Schyler and I differ."

"Better watch it, Thea," Sam said. "Schyler's technique married to Scotty's sincerity. It's a dangerous combination."

"What's dangerous?" Evvie asked, walking into the kitchen. "Thanks for kicking me, Thea. I'm going to limp all day." She joined Sam by the kitchen counter, and they exchanged morning kisses.

"The Hugheses' way with women," Sam said. "Scotty's been showing his stuff."

"It can't be that potent," Scotty said. "Evvie picked you over Schyler."

"Yes, but I'm crazy," Evvie said. "We all know that. How's Schyler doing? Does he like Brown?"

"He seems to," Scotty replied. "He makes a lot of Brownie jokes, keeps waiting to run into the Girl Scout of his dreams."

"Oh, dear," Meg said. "People warned me that this was what having teenagers in the house would be like. Sex at the breakfast table."

"And other places," Sam said.

"Sam!" Evvie said, giving him a swat. "Megs, how does the day shape up? Where are Nicky and Clark?"

"Nicky took Clark to see the factory," Meg replied. "Nicky's putting together a deal to convert a factory into condominiums," she explained. "As far as the rest of the day goes, dinner's scheduled for two. Thea, do you know when Gina's going to get here?"

"Around one," Thea said. "And they want her back at the hospital by four."

"Maybe we should move dinner up to one-thirty, then," Meg said. "I don't want to rush things."

"What can I do to help?" Sam asked.

"Use him, Megs," Evvie said. "I want Sam thoroughly housebroken before we get married."

"You're not getting married for four years," Meg pointed out. "He doesn't have to start learning domestic skills in my kitchen."

"I'm full of domestic skills," Sam protested. "My grandmother's seen to that. I can vacuum and sew buttons and make scrambled eggs."

"That's more than I can do," Scotty said.

"That's more than Evvie can do," Sam said.

"It's against my religion to thread a needle," Evvie said. "Besides, why should I sew buttons when Sam does it so well. He sews my buttons, and I give him endless sisters in exchange. It all works out equitably."

"What's equitable?" Sybil asked, entering the kitchen. "Is there anything for breakfast?"

"Serve-yourself," Meg said. "Morning, sweetie."

"Morning," Sybil said, promptly putting bread in the toaster. "Hi, Sam. Want to help me look for candy wrappers?"

119

"I thought you'd already found your hundred," Thea said.

"I did," Sybil replied. "And I mailed them off weeks ago. But then it occurred to me I could send in another hundred in Evvie's name. She has a whole different address, and I trust her with my money. I need thirty-two more wrappers, and I only have six days to find them."

"A woman with a mission," Sam said. "I'd be delighted to go wrapper hunting with you."

"Not today," Meg said. "There's too much to be done here. I've already made the pumpkin pie, but the apple pie still has to get baked. Scotty and Thea, I want you to peel the apples. Sybil, you're going to help me make the stuffing. And Sam and Evvie are in charge of setting up the dining room."

"What does Claire get to do?" Thea asked. "Besides sleep all day."

"Claire's going to make the salad," Meg said. "Clark's making the salad dressing, and all the other vegetables. I'm baking the bread and the pies."

"That leaves the turkey," Evvie pointed out.

"Sam's young and strong," Meg said. "He can load and unload the turkey. Nicky'll carve, of course."

"Sounds like a perfect division of labor," Scotty said. "If you'll show me to the apples, I'm ready to work."

And by the time Nicky and Claire got home they all were working, doing their jobs in happy confusion. Thea couldn't imagine a more perfect Thanksgiving. Nicky's pleasure at being surrounded by family and friends was palpable. Megs clearly took joy in the beauty of her dining room, with its fresh coat of paint and its newly purchased antique oak dining room table and chairs. Thea and Sybil shared the responsibility of washing the good china and crystal, which Evvie and Sam then carried into the dining room. Nicky and Clark debated over which bottles of wine should be served. Claire sliced cucumbers and tomatoes, and worried noisily about her fingernails. Scotty moved chairs around and offered his services to anyone with two hands and three tasks. The house smelt wonderful from all the good foods being cooked, and everyone was laughing at one joke or another. Thea wished she could preserve the day forever.

Kip and his family arrived on schedule. He carried Gina in his arms, and once again, Thea was taken aback by how small and frail Gina was. In the past month, the leukemia had obviously gotten worse, but Gina was clearly thrilled to be out of the hospital, to be at Thea's house for Thanksgiving.

Neither Mrs. Dozier nor Dani seemed nearly as pleased to be there. Thea had seen Dani at school, where she had a kind of trampy charm to her, but today she'd troweled the makeup on, and it was hard to see that there was a pretty fifteen-year-old buried under the cosmetics. Mrs. Dozier simply looked ill at ease.

But Nicky was determined to be the perfect host, and once he got the Doziers settled into the living room, they had no choice but to relax, get comfortable, become part of the occasion. Thea was chased out of the kitchen, and she joined them in the living room.

"Can I see your bedroom?" Gina asked. "I want to see your room and Sybil's."

"They're upstairs," Thea said. "That's a long distance for Kip to carry you."

"I'll help," Scotty said. "If it's all right with Kip. We can turn ourselves into a human ski lift and carry Gina between us."

"Sounds good to me," Kip said. They shared Gina's weight and carried her carefully up the stairs.

"I can walk," Gina told Scotty. "I'm not crippled."

"But this way you look like a queen," Scotty said. "You know Gina is a nickname for Regina, and Regina means queen."

"I didn't know that," Gina said to Kip. "You never told me that."

"It slipped my mind," Kip said.

"From now on don't call me pumpkin," Gina said. "Call me queen."

"Pumpkin queen," Kip said. "Who's bedroom is this?"

"Sybil and Claire's," Thea replied. "It's not my style." At least it isn't red, she thought. Claire had insisted on red bedrooms for three years running.

"It's pretty," Gina said. "Now let me see yours."

So Thea led them to her bedroom. Gina smiled as soon as she saw it. "This is what I want my room to look like," she declared. "Just like this, with lace curtains and teddy bears and all those pretty pictures."

"It is pretty," Kip said.

"You've never seen it?" Scotty asked.

"No," Kip said. "I've only been here once."

Scotty smiled. Thea looked at him and Kip and wished she was the one they were carrying.

"Had enough of the tour?" Kip asked Gina.

"Yes," Gina said. "Carry me down all by yourself, Kip."

"Sure," Kip said. He and Scotty shifted positions, and they proceeded downstairs.

Thea was delighted to see Nicky, Clark, and Mrs. Dozier sitting in the living room together, obviously exchanging comfortable small talk. Dani was in the dining room, eyeing Sam. If Evvie minded, it didn't show.

Claire sat next to Gina on the sofa, and got into a

conversation with her about the latest issue of *TV Dreamstars*. Sybil and Megs were building a fire in the rarely used fireplace. Thea stood at the dining room doorway and smiled.

"This is very nice of your family," Kip said. "To have us here."

"It's nice of you to come," Thea replied. "Doesn't everything look perfect?"

"It sure does," Kip said. "You know, even before Gina got sick, we never had a Thanksgiving like this."

"Neither have we," Evvie said as she and Sam walked over to them. "All this hoopla is a first for us, too."

"Thanksgivings were always deadly in my home," Sam said. "It was just me and my grandparents, so there was nothing special about it."

"You grew up with your grandparents?" Kip asked.

Sam nodded. "They're very nice people," he declared. "But on holidays, you want more."

"You want what they have on TV," Kip said. "You want all this."

"I know," Evvie said. "This is just a television Thanksgiving. I feel like I'm in a *Star Trek* episode. You know, the kind where everything looks like what it's supposed to be, but it's really just a facade."

"What do you mean?" Kip asked.

"This is so much Nicky's idea of Thanksgiving," Evvie declared. "Megs's, too, for that matter. She spent her Thanksgivings with Aunt Grace."

"The Spanish Inquisition was probably more fun," Sam said.

"But it's all so storybook perfect," Evvie said. "The turkey and the pies and Megs's grandmother's china. There's no reality to any of this."

123

"That turkey had better be real," Sam said. "I'm starving."

"There must be something for you to nosh," Evvie said. "Go check in the kitchen." She kissed Sam good-bye as he left the room, and then she turned to her sister. "Nosh," she said. "I now know thirty-two different Yiddish words and expressions, except I still get kibitz and kibbutz mixed up."

"Oops," Sam said, walking rapidly back into the dining room. "Uh, Kip, I didn't realize your sister knew Scotty."

"She doesn't," Kip said.

"Oh," Sam said, trying not to grin. "She certainly is the friendly type, then."

"I'll kill her," Kip said, and he ran into the kitchen. Thea could hear Dani's muffled protests, and what sounded like an embarrassed apology from Scotty. It was hard to tell, since Sam was laughing. In a moment, Scotty joined them in the dining room, wiping lipstick off most of his face. Sam kept laughing.

"Men," Evvie said to Thea. "Is Dani safe in there?"

"I don't know," Thea said. It took courage, but she walked into the kitchen to see how things were. Dani was standing against the kitchen door, and Kip was inches away from her, whispering angrily.

"Kip, relax," Thea said, putting her hand on his shoulder.

Kip whirled around, and for a moment Thea thought he was going to hit her. "This is family," he said. "Leave us alone."

"Calm down," Thea said. "Nobody got hurt."

"What do you know?" Kip asked her.

"I know you're getting angry over very little," Thea

said. "I know if you don't calm down, you're going to ruin Thanksgiving for everybody. Megs is going to be back here any minute, and you don't want her to see you like this."

"I'm not through with you, Dani," Kip said, but he moved away from her, allowing her to inch out. Dani smirked, then sauntered out of the kitchen. "I'm sorry," Kip said to Thea. "I told Dani she had to behave herself, but I guess she figured that meant throwing herself at boys and not men."

"Good," Thea said. "Clark wouldn't stand a chance against her. Now wash your face with cold water, and let's join everyone else."

Kip followed her instructions, and walked with her to the living room.

"Daisy, isn't it time we began serving dinner?" Nick asked. "I, for one, am famished."

"I, for two, am famished," Dani said.

"Come on, Kip," Nick said. "Why don't we go into the kitchen and start carrying things out. Daisy, come with us and show us what to take."

"No!" Gina said. "I don't want Kip to go."

"He's only going to the kitchen," Nick said. "Come on. Why don't we get you settled into the dining room, and then you'll be able to see Kip in the kitchen."

"I don't feel good," Gina said.

Kip immediately went to her side. "What's the matter?" he asked.

"It's so cold," Gina said. "Why is it so cold?"

Kip felt her forehead. "She's running a fever," he said. "We'd better get her back right away."

"Maybe it's just the excitement," Clark said. "Why don't we wait a few minutes, and see how Gina feels then."

125

"We can't take that chance," Kip said. "Thea, I'm sorry, but we've got to go."

"I know," Thea said.

"Dani, call the cab company," Kip said. "Mom, get the coats. We're leaving now."

"I don't want to leave," Dani said. "Just because stupid Gina's sick again doesn't mean I have to go, too."

"Don't worry about a cab," Nick said. "I'll drive you to the hospital."

"Kip, I'm scared!" Gina cried. "I wanna go home."

"Mom, get the goddam coats," Kip said. "Dani, move it. Thanks for the lift, Mr. Sebastian. Relax, Gina, and don't worry. We'll get you back to the hospital right away."

"I hurt all over," Gina said. "Kip?"

"I'm right here, pumpkin," Kip said. He lifted Gina off the sofa and with Sam's help carried her out of the house. Dani and Mrs. Dozier trailed behind him. Mrs. Dozier was crying.

Thea followed them to the car. She'd left her coat behind, and it was cold outside. "Do you want me to go with you?" she asked.

"Don't bother," Kip said. "Stay with your family."

"I'll be back in a few minutes," Nick said. "Relax, everyone. We'll get Gina back to the hospital in no time."

"Thank you, Mr. Sebastian," Mrs. Dozier said. "You're a true gentleman."

"Why do I have to leave?" Dani asked. Thea couldn't hear the reply because Nicky had turned the ignition on. He began backing the car out of the driveway. She stood outside watching them drive off, and then opened the kitchen door and walked back in.

"I feel awful," Meg said, and she put her arm around

Thea's shoulder. "Do you think it was too much for her, coming here today?"

"The doctors wouldn't have let her come if they'd thought she was too ill," Clark said.

What do you know, Thea thought, but there was no point in confronting Clark. He was only trying to make Megs feel better. That was Clark's primary function in life, at least the way he saw it.

"She must be very weak for Kip to have moved so quickly," Sam said. "She can't have much time left."

"Weeks," Thea replied, praying it was that long. Only Megs's embrace kept her from weeping.

"It was dumb of her to come," Sybil declared. "She's sick and sick people should stay in the hospital."

"And leave healthy people alone?" Thea asked.

"It wasn't my idea to have her come," Sybil replied. "Now, maybe she'll die."

"I'm sorry," Scotty said. "She might have gotten upset because Kip got angry."

"About what?" Claire asked.

"About none of your business," Thea said.

"I'm going to find out eventually," Claire said. "You might as well tell me now."

"You might as well stop snooping," Thea shouted.

Evvie looked at her family and friends. "Next year," she said to Sam, "Thanksgiving at your grandparents'."

CHAPTER ELEVEN

Thea panicked when she found Gina's bed empty. Her first thought was that Gina had died and no one had thought to tell her. Who was she supposed to ask?

She looked around the ward, but couldn't force herself to ask the other kids. So she walked to the corridor and found a nurse.

"They moved Gina," the nurse told her. "She's in room fourteen B."

"She's worse," Thea said. There was no point in phrasing it as a question.

The nurse nodded. "She won't be coming back here," she said. "Her family is with her now."

Thea nodded and found her way to 14B. Dani was sitting outside the room. "It's you," she said. "Still mad about yesterday?"

"I wasn't mad," Thea told her. "How's Gina?"

"Croaking," Dani said with a shrug. "Same as always. Kip's in there with her. I guess you're here to see him."

"I guess so," Thea replied. "Can I go in?"

"Sure," Dani said. "But be careful. It smells of death in there."

Thea wanted to ask how Dani knew what death smelled like, but as soon as she opened the door, she could see what Dani meant. It was a room for dying, and its air was different, more oppressive than the rest of the hospital.

"Dani said I could come in," she whispered to Kip. He was sitting by Gina's bed, holding her hand.

Kip nodded. Gina was sleeping or unconscious. Thea couldn't be sure which. She was pale, and the only sign of life left in her was her feverish condition, the sweat on her forehead, the occasional, almost angry, jerks her body made.

"Where's your mother?" Thea asked. Megs would be there with her daughter, she knew.

"Out somewhere," Kip said. "I don't know."

"How are you doing?" Thea asked.

"I'm fine," he replied. "We're all fine. Sorry about yesterday."

"Don't worry about it," Thea said. She reached over and touched his hand, but Kip didn't seem to notice. "Have you gotten any sleep since yesterday?"

"She sleeps better when I'm in the room," Kip said. "I nod off occasionally. It isn't for that much longer."

"What happened?" Thea asked. "It wasn't because of us, was it?"

Kip shook his head. "She shouldn't have gone," he said. "But we knew that at the time. We just all denied it. The doctors, too. We wanted her to have that . . . that last taste of normalcy. But she's been getting weaker and weaker."

"I'm sorry," Thea said.

"Don't be," Kip said. "At least I won't have to buy any Christmas presents."

"Oh, Kip," Thea said, and the sound of her voice roused Gina.

"Dani?" she whispered.

"No, honey, it's me," Thea said. "Thea. Do you want to see Dani? She's right outside."

"Thea," Gina said. She reached for Thea, who gave her her hand to hold. Gina's touch was terrifying, filled with sickness. Thea marveled that Kip could sit there holding her hand without flinching.

"I wanted to see you," Thea said. "We worried about you yesterday."

Kip shook his head. "Gina doesn't remember about yesterday," he said.

"How's Sybil?" Gina asked, and her voice gained strength, and sounded almost normal.

"She's fine," Thea said. "She's at home collecting candy wrappers. I told you about the wrappers."

"Sybil," Gina said. She closed her eyes, and Thea thought she'd drifted off again. "Angels in heaven like Sybil," she murmured.

"Beautiful angels," Thea said. "Just like you."

"Mommy's gone," Gina said. "Daddy's gone. Just you and Sybil and angels."

"Kip's here," Thea said. "See, he's sitting right by you, holding your hand."

"Kip," Gina said. "Kip and Thea and angels. I like angels. They're pretty."

"So are you," Thea said. She had no idea what she

was saying or even why. Megs could handle this, she thought, and I'm like Megs. "You're so pretty, Gina, and so sweet. I love you, you know."

Gina seemed to nod. "Angels," she said. "Angels in heaven with me." Her breathing became heavier, and Thea saw that she was sleeping again.

"She drifts in and out," Kip said. "So do Mom and Dani."

"Is there anything I can do?" Thea asked.

"No," Kip said. "Frankly, I'm surprised you even bothered showing up."

"Kip, don't do that," Thea said. "I'm part of this, and you damn well know it."

"Yeah," Kip said. "You might as well go now. And if you see Dani out there, tell her to get Mom. I sent her to the cafeteria an hour ago, but there's a chance she might still be there."

"I'll tell her," Thea said, but when she left the room, Dani was nowhere to be seen. So Thea walked to the cafeteria and found Dani and her mother together.

"Kip thinks you should go back now," she said to Mrs. Dozier. She felt presumptuous, but there was no other way for Kip's message to be delivered.

Mrs. Dozier nodded. She looked accustomed to being bullied. "I will in a minute," she said. "Let me finish my coffee."

"Don't rush on her account, Ma," Dani said. "She's nobody to tell you what to do."

"It's for Kip," Mrs. Dozier said. "He wants me there."

"That makes it all right, then," Dani said. "Whatever Kip wants, Kip gets."

Thea resisted the urge to slug Dani. "I'm going home

now," she said to Mrs. Dozier. "Please call me if there's anything I can do."

"Thank you," Mrs. Dozier said, and to Thea's surprise, she took Thea's hand and squeezed it. "You've been so sweet to us, so understanding."

"She's a saint," Dani said.

"Compared to you she is," Mrs. Dozier said. "Please, when all this is over with, come for supper sometime."

"All right," Thea said. "I have to go now. I'll see you later."

"You're an angel," Mrs. Dozier called after her, but Thea didn't turn around. She walked as fast as she could out of the hospital, and then jogged the rest of the way home.

Her house was still bustling with guests and activities, and Thea felt as alien there as she had in the hospital room. Sybil was putting on her jacket as Thea walked in. "Where are you going?" Thea asked.

"On the great candy-wrapper hunt," Sybil replied. "Sam's coming with me."

"May I join you?" Thea asked. "I have great eyes for candy wrappers."

Sybil scowled. "Too many people and we'll all end up talking and not looking," she said.

"I promise I'll look," Thea said.

"Tell you what," Scotty said, joining them in the hallway. "I'll walk with Thea and look with her while you and Sam look together. How's that, Sybil?"

Sybil grinned. "Fine," she said. "Sam, come on!"

"Coming!" Sam called, and soon the four of them were on the expedition together.

"We're going to Oak Hollow Road," Sybil declared.

"Lots of kids walk there, and I found a lot of wrappers there in October."

"Sounds promising," Sam said.

"This should work out really well," Sybil said. "See, there's Oak Hollow up ahead. Scotty, you and Thea walk to the left, and Sam and I'll walk to the right."

"I bet we'll find more wrappers than you do," Thea said.

"You will not," Sybil said. She grabbed Sam's arm and pulled him with her. "Come on, Sam," she said. "Let's find a thousand wrappers."

"Come on, Scotty," Thea said. "Let's find a thousand and one." She heard herself laughing, and couldn't believe that she was. An hour ago, she'd been sitting with Gina, watching her die, and now she was outside searching the sides of the road for garbage. She loved Gina, probably more than Dani did, and yet she was outside laughing. No wonder Kip had been surprised she'd shown up.

"Penny for your thoughts," Scotty said.

"You don't want them," Thea replied.

"That little girl," Scotty said. "She's dying, right?"

Thea nodded.

"A kid I went to school with died," Scotty said. "I'd known him since, I don't know, since fourth grade, I guess. That's when we both started Mayfield Academy. And when you go to prep school like that, you really know the other kids, because you live together in the dorm. Not that this guy was a big friend of mine or anything, but he was someone I knew. Someone I ate with. Someone I heard crying when he was homesick. I guess he heard me cry, too, on occasion."

Thea liked the sound of Scotty's voice, and was glad she didn't have to look at him. She stared down at the side of the road and searched for wrappers while he spoke.

"Anyway, about three years ago, they found out he had cancer," Scotty said. "Brain tumor. Real fast. Real bad. He was dead six months later. But it was all during the school year. He had a seizure right before Halloween, and he was dead by Easter break. Of course, once he went into the hospital, he was out of school, but they made us visit him. He looked weird, his hair all shaved off, big bandage around his head. The next time we saw him, he looked worse, and the third time, you knew he was a goner."

"Did you go to the funeral?" Thea asked. There. Now she'd said the *f* word, too.

"We had to," Scotty replied. "None of us wanted to, but they bused us to the church. His mother cried. His parents were divorced, and his father couldn't make it, but his mother cried, and she said what made it all worthwhile was seeing us all there. Like that proved the guy was popular. I mean, he was, but it wasn't like we were all his friends. We had to go. I had to go. That's the only funeral I've ever been to. You ever go to one?"

"Not yet," Thea said. If she looked hard enough for wrappers, she wouldn't start crying.

"Boring," Scotty declared. "Lots of talk about heaven. When I die, I don't want a funeral. Schyler says he wants a big one, with all his old girlfriends there, but not me. Just cremate me and scatter my ashes."

"Where?" Thea asked.

"On Wall Street," Scotty replied. "In the Stock Exchange."

Thea laughed. Scotty was silent for a moment, and then he laughed, too.

"You have a wonderful laugh," he said. "You should laugh more often."

"I laugh all the time," Thea said. "Just not lately. You picked a bad weekend to hear me laugh."

"Can I have another chance some other weekend?" Scotty asked.

"Do you mean can you come for another visit?" Thea asked. "Sure. Now that Nicky and Megs are in the inviting habit, I bet they'd be delighted to have you come back."

"Good," Scotty said. "Because I want to keep seeing you."

"You do?" Thea said. "Why?"

"Oh, come on now," Scotty said. "You've got to know how pretty you are. Girls as pretty as you always know."

"Oh," Thea said. She knew she used to look in the mirror and admire herself, but lately she'd had other things on her mind. "Am I as pretty as Dani?"

"Dani," Scotty grunted. "I knew you'd bring that up."

"It's a natural enough question," Thea said. "Oh, good. I found a Wattabar wrapper. It's in mint condition, too."

"Dani means nothing to me," Scotty declared.

"I never doubted that," Thea said. "Your courtship was pretty brief, if fervent."

"She practically raped me," Scotty said. "I was standing in the kitchen, minding my own business, and she walked over to me and started kissing. Ordinarily I would have told her to stop, but I was a guest in your house, and I thought that might be rude. Maybe I was supposed to kiss her, so I did. My mother brought me up to do whatever my hosts did. And your parents kiss, and so do Evvie and Sam. I figured that was how you did things here, so I kissed Dani back. But I certainly wouldn't have started if she hadn't. There's a Yummie Junior. Sybil's collecting those, right?"

"Right," Thea said. "Oh, here's an Mmm Mmms with Almonds. Yuck. It has ants on it."

"I'll brush them off for you," Scotty said, and he took the wrapper from Thea and delicately removed the ants. "I think I'm in love with you, Thea Sebastian," he said, and, wrappers in hand, kissed her.

"What?" Thea said when he'd finished.

"You heard me," Scotty said "I know you don't love me yet, but you will, I promise."

Thea stared at Scotty and then checked to see if Sam and Sybil were within earshot. But they were already a few hundred feet away, and engrossed in their own conversation.

"Scotty," Thea said. "I don't love you. You don't love me, either. Hold on. I think I see a Sweet Somethings wrapper over there."

"In your family, everyone falls in love fast," Scotty said. "I know all about it. It's all Clark ever talks about. How your mother fell in love with your father, and then Evvie with Sam. And now you and me. I can see why you might not have known it at first, because you have had other things on your mind, but soon you'll realize it and then we'll be together."

"Excuse me," Thea said. "But there's an Mmm Mmm wrapper under that stone."

"Forget the wrapper," Scotty said. "And listen to me. I could have played this the traditional way, dates, letters, yearning phone calls. But I couldn't afford to take the chance. You obviously feel something for Kip, even if it is one-sided, and I know it's hard for you, his sister dying and all, and I'm only here until Sunday. Besides, things are crowded in your house. All those sisters. And Sam. Schyler was right when he said Sam has a gift for getting in the way. So I'm telling you now, and years from now you'll look back at this moment, and remember us on Oak Creek Road and wonder how you ever could have doubted."

"Oak Hollow Road," Thea said. "What makes you say my feelings for Kip are one-sided?"

"You'll get over him," Scotty said. "He isn't worthy of you, anyway. I'm going to be a millionaire, Thea, by the time I'm twenty-five. And after that, I'm only going to get richer. I'll buy you anything you want."

"You have the wrong sister," Thea said. "Try that line on Claire."

"She's not my type," Scotty replied. "She reminds me too much of Schyler. I saw you Wednesday night, and I thought, there she is, the girl I've always dreamed of. Thea Sebastian. Thea Sebastian Hughes. That's perfect. Sebastian's my grandfather's name, you know."

"No, I didn't," Thea said. "Scotty, you're very sweet, but I'm not in the mood to be proposed to right now."

"Let me know when," he said. "I'll give you roses."

"I'd rather have candy wrappers," Thea said. "Oh, good. Here's another Wattabar. You want to brush off its ants for me?"

"The first test of my love," Scotty said. He shook the wrapper free of the ants, and then, while handing it to Thea, kissed her again. Why not, Thea thought, and kissed him back. In her family, they did fall in love at first sight. Maybe if she'd bothered to look at Scotty two nights ago, she might have fallen in love, too.

She was hardly aware of the car whizzing past them. It

only penetrated her consciousness when she realized someone might have seen them kissing. Kip, Thea thought, although she knew he didn't have a car, and was unlikely to be anywhere near Oak Hollow Road. But the thought of him made her aware of the car, and the car made her think of Sybil, and she looked over to the side of the road where Sybil was standing, and somehow, as though she knew what she was going to see, she watched the car race toward Sybil. And Thea began to scream, but the car was making too much noise, only Scotty could hear her, and he turned and saw, too, as the car hit Sybil and she flew into the air and the car kept going faster and faster and Sam was standing there, and Sybil was on the ground, and the wrappers, the damn candy wrappers started floating down, landing on the road, landing on Sybil lying on the road.

"SYBIL!" Thea screamed again, and this time they all could hear her, but it was too late. She ran the yards to Sybil's side, and Scotty followed her, dropping his wrappers. We'll have to retrieve them, Thea thought. The wrappers. Sybil's going to want the wrappers.

"My God," Scotty said as he reached Sam and looked down at Sybil. "Is she alive?"

"I don't know," Sam said. "I . . . I haven't checked yet."

"Checked?" Thea shouted. At least she meant to shout. She wasn't sure she actually said anything, but her lips were moving, and she was thinking checked and candy wrappers and Sybil and alive.

Scotty bent down. "She's still breathing," he said. "We'd better not move her, though."

"Here's my jacket," Sam said. He took it off, and draped it over Sybil. "Thea, we need to call an ambulance."

138

"The car hit her," Thea said. "Did you see that?"

"We saw it," Scotty said. He took his jacket off as well, and put it on Sybil. Thea couldn't get over how silly Sybil looked, lying on the road, covered by jackets and candy wrappers.

"Wake up," Thea said. "She hates waking up in the morning. Sybil, wake up."

"You take Thea," Sam said. "Find a phone fast. I'll stay here with Sybil."

"All right," Scotty said. He put his left arm around Thea, but this time she knew he wasn't going to kiss her, and then they walked down the road, turned on Old Mill Road, walked until they found a house, and then walked to the house, rang the bell, begged for entry, explained what had happened. Thea listened while Scotty talked.

"Accident. Hit-and-run. Twelve-year-old."

"No," Thea said. "Sybil. It was Sybil." And she started crying, and didn't stop, not even when they ushered her into the living room, and didn't stop until she heard the ambulance wail its arrival, and watched as they carefully lifted Sybil off the road, and drove her away, to the hospital, to safety, to a place which made people well—or watched while they died.

CHAPTER TWELVE

It was almost as though they'd moved the weekend party into the surgical waiting room, Thea thought. Everyone was there, except Sybil of course. Sam and Evvie were huddled on the floor, and Claire was sitting close enough to them that Evvie could occasionally reach out and stroke her hair. Nicky and Megs were sitting on a sofa, their faces devoid of expression; but their bodies and their thoughts seemed merged, as though by their unity, they could hold the world together. Clark paced, fidgeted, brought coffee and sandwiches, made phone calls, tried to be useful, and succeeded only in not being invisible. Scotty sat by Thea's side. Thea didn't know why. Maybe it was because they had witnessed the accident together. Maybe it was because he loved her. She was hardly conscious of him, and didn't care what his motives were.

There had been chaos in the emergency room, Nicky hysterical with grief, Megs close to paralysis from shock. Clark had been helpful then, and the doctors had known what to do, how to calm people down so forms could be filled out, information could be obtained. Nicky had stopped shaking long enough to sign consent forms for surgery. Within two hours of the accident, Sybil was on the operating table, and all Thea knew was that the longer they took, the longer Sybil continued to live.

"Come on, girls," Clark said, sometime after the third hour. "You must be hungry. You need a break. Let's go to the cafeteria and get something to eat."

"No," Thea said. She remembered Mrs. Dozier sitting in the cafeteria, and couldn't bear the thought of facing her again. Not that Mrs. Dozier was likely to still be there. But Thea wasn't taking any chances.

"Claire, come with me," Clark pleaded. "It isn't healthy for you to be sitting so still. And you're not doing Sybil any good by starving yourself."

"I'm not leaving," Claire said.

"We're fine, Clark," Evvie said. "Why don't you go down and bring us back something. We just can't leave right now."

"All right," Clark said. "Scotty, come with me. I'll need the extra set of hands."

So Scotty got up and joined Clark. Thea felt relieved when they were gone. They didn't belong. They weren't family.

Sam turned to Thea. "I thought I heard you scream," he said. "Did you?"

Thea nodded. "I saw the car coming," she replied. She could see it again and again, each time in her memory getting larger, and the arc of Sybil's flight growing higher and more delicate. After five hours, it was almost poetry the way Sybil flew and descended, and the candy wrappers looked almost like flower petals.

"I reached for her," Sam said. "I remember that. I reached for her, tried to pull her out of the way, but it was too late."

"Sam, don't," Evvie said. "It wasn't your fault."

"I don't know," he said. "There should have been something I could do."

"There was nothing," Thea said. "Cars speed on Oak Hollow Road. That's one reason why people drive there, so they can speed."

"I didn't know that," Meg said. "About the speeding."

Thea nodded. "The car was going very fast," she said.

"No, I mean that cars always speeded there," Meg said. "If I'd known that, I never would have let Sybil go there."

"There was no way you could know that," Nick declared. "Daisy, don't blame yourself. Some hit-and-run driver hurt Sybil, not you."

"Not you," Evvie echoed, holding onto Sam.

"She's so young," Meg said. "Only twelve."

"She's strong," Nick said. "And she's not a quitter. When Sybil sets her mind to something, she always accomplishes it."

Megs began to cry. "She's my baby," she said, and Nicky held on to her, while she wept.

"She'll be all right, Megs," Claire said. "I know it. Sybil isn't going to die."

"She can't die," Nick said. "She can't."

Angels like Sybil, Thea thought. Gina had asked after her. Had Gina known what was going to happen? Did the dying know who the dying were going to be?

Clark and Scotty came back with boxes filled with coffee and soup, sandwiches and fruit. Thea stared at the sandwich Scotty gave her. Evvie nibbled on hers. Megs continued to cry.

"Nick, maybe we should get Meg out of here," Clark suggested. "Find a room for her to lie down in."

"No," Nick said, and he held on to Megs even more tightly.

"They were selling Yummie Juniors in the cafeteria," Scotty declared. "They had a vending machine with them. I almost bought one."

"They're awful," Claire said. "They stick in your teeth for hours."

"I know," Scotty said. "That's why I didn't get any."

Thea thought about how much Sybil hated hospitals. It didn't seem fair that she should be in one.

A police officer came by, and asked Scotty, Thea, and Sam for statements again. They'd already told what they knew back in the emergency room, but the officer wanted to hear it again. Color and description of car. Had they seen the driver at all? What about the license plate? They told him what they remembered, which wasn't much, and went back to sitting on the floor, playing with the food, talking about Yummie Juniors.

"There's turkey at home," Meg said. "We had so much extra because the Doziers didn't stay."

"They wanted to," Thea said. "They apologized for leaving."

"I know," Meg said. "How is Gina?"

Thea shrugged. Dying wasn't a word she cared to say out loud.

"Maybe I'll have a turkey sandwich when I get home," Evvie said. "Sam, would you like a sandwich?"

"That'll be good," Sam replied. "We can make sandwiches for everybody."

"I can help," Scotty said.

"Fine," Sam said. "The three of us will make sandwiches later."

Time passed in silence. At one point Evvie asked Sam what he had done with her psychology textbook. At another, Claire asked Scotty how many boys there were in his school. Megs and Nicky turned back into themselves. Clark continued to fuss. Thea sat there and pictured the car, the flight, the showering of wrappers. She no longer was sure what color the car had been, although she'd known at the time it was blue.

After five hours, the surgeon came out. He walked over to Nicky and Megs, but all the others could hear him. "She's still with us," he said. "The internal injuries were extensive, and there was a lot of blood lost. We had to remove her spleen, but she can live with that. And there's no sign of permanent neurological disfunction."

Nicky nodded.

"The next twenty-four hours are critical," the doctor said. "The risk of infection is great, and the bleeding could start again."

"Then what?" Nick asked. "When she makes it through."

"There was a lot of damage to the legs and knees," the doctor said. "We patched what we could, but our first concern had to be to stop the bleeding. She's a strong little girl, and her functions are good, blood pressure is stable, she's putting out urine. Let's get her through the next few days, and then you can start talking with the orthopedic surgeon about what lies ahead."

"Can we see her?" Meg asked.

"Only for a moment," the doctor said. "She's in post-op. Just her parents."

Megs nodded. She and Nicky rose, and followed the doctor to Sybil.

"We should give blood," Sam said. "Tomorrow, let's all give blood. Even if it's not Sybil's type,. we should all do it."

"Good idea," Clark said. "And once Meg and Nick get back here, we should all go home. We won't do Sybil any good by staying here. She needs us healthy and well rested for tomorrow."

Evvie nodded. "Clark's right," she said. "I don't know what Nicky and Megs are going to do, but we might as well leave. Tomorrow is going to be a very long day."

"It can't be any longer than today," Thea said. She got up and stretched and was amazed to discover just how badly her body ached. Scotty got up with her, and massaged her shoulders. Thea thought she would cry with gratitude.

Nicky and Megs returned after a few minutes. "She's sleeping," Meg said. "She's very pale, and they have her wired up a thousand different ways."

"We're going to go home," Evvie declared. "Do you want to join us?"

"Later," Nick said. "We want to talk to the doctors some more. And they might let us see Sybil again if we stay."

"We'll see you at home, then," Evvie said. She walked over to her parents, and kissed them. "Call us if you need anything."

"Thank you, darling," Meg said. But Thea felt Megs and Nicky withdraw into their own world as the rest of them picked up their jackets and bags and began the procession home.

There was something comforting about being in the house again, even without Nicky and Megs and Sybil. Scotty and Sam cut up the turkey for sandwiches. Claire sliced bread, and Clark threw together a salad. Thea set the table, and Evvie brewed tea. Soon they'd created an instant feast, and if almost none of them ate anything, it still felt better to have shared in the preparations.

Nicky and Megs got home around ten. "We saw Sybil again," Meg said, hanging her coat in the hall closet. "She looked better, I think, more color in her cheeks."

"She's going to be fine," Nick declared. "I think she knew we were there, too. I saw her open her eyes, just for a moment, and look at us."

"I didn't see that," Meg admitted. "But Nicky swears she did."

"Good," Clark said. "There's plenty of food, if you'd like some."

"Not just now," Meg said. "Thank you, Clark."

"The doctors say every minute she's alive is a minute she's getting stronger," Nick said. "She's still not past the crisis point, but they said there's every reason to hope."

"Thank God," Clark said. "Are you sure you wouldn't like some tea?"

"Tea sounds good," Meg said.

So Clark ran into the kitchen and brought out two mugs of tea. Megs sipped hers, and Nicky ignored his.

"I called my grandfather," Sam said. "He's a surgeon, heart surgeon, but I asked him to find out the names of top orthopedic surgeons in the area. He said he'd get back to me tomorrow. He also said the hospital here was excellent, and he was sure Sybil was getting the best possible care."

"Thank you, Sam," Meg said. "That was very thoughtful of you."

"I wish I could do more," he replied.

Clark took a deep breath. "This is going to cost a lot of money," he said. "I know you're not ready to start thinking about that, Nick, but the cost is going to add up. How's your health insurance?"

"What health insurance," Nick replied.

Thea could see the shock in Clark's face. "You're kidding," he said. "Nick, this could run into the hundreds of thousands."

"Let it," Nick said. "We'll find a way."

"Let me help," Clark said. "I have more money than I know what to do with. I can pick up the costs."

"That's very sweet, Clark," Meg said. "But it isn't necessary."

Thea realized her parents had already begun discussing the money situation. She saw Megs put a hand on Nicky's arm, as though to restrain him.

"Meg, dearest, this is no time for pride," Clark said. "You can't possibly afford the sorts of medical bills you're going to be facing."

"It's none of your concern," Nick declared. "It's a family problem. We'll solve it by ourselves."

"Don't be an idiot, Sebastian," Clark said, his face flushed. "You can't let Meg and your daughters suffer because of your stupid outsider's pride."

"And you can't buy your way into this family," Nick said. "Money isn't going to make you Daisy's husband, or the father of my children. So forget it."

"We'll manage," Meg said. "We always have before, and we will again."

"What about Aunt Grace?" Thea asked.

"No," Nick said. "We've never taken a penny from her, and we're not about to start now."

"I can leave Harvard," Evvie said. "I don't know if we can get our money back for this semester, but at least we won't have to pay for next."

"No," Sam said. "Don't be ridiculous, Evvie. I'll ask my grandparents to pay for you. I'm sure they will."

"Stop it, all of you," Meg said. "Sam, Clark, Evvie, I understand your concerns, and you're really very sweet, but right now the important thing is for Sybil just to make it through the night. Don't you understand that? We have to take this one day at a time, and right now all that matters is Sybil getting stronger. The money is secondary."

"I'm sorry," Evvie said. "Megs, you must be exhausted. Why don't you rest for a little while? You, too, Nicky. There's a phone in your room, you'll be sure to know if the hospital calls."

"Will you girls go to sleep?" Meg asked.

"After we clean up," Evvie replied. "I promise."

"All right then," Meg said. "Come on, Nicky. Let's get some rest."

Nicky followed Megs upstairs. The others busied themselves with washing dishes and putting things away, and then went to their respective bedrooms.

"I'm not going to be able to sleep," Thea said as she stretched out by Evvie's side. "I keep picturing the accident, the way Sybil looked."

"It's all right," Evvie said. "You don't have to sleep.

Nicky and Megs aren't sleeping. I doubt that Sam is, either. But just resting will help."

"She isn't going to die," Claire said. "I know Sybil, better than any of you, and she isn't going to die."

"I agree," Evvie said.

"But the rest," Claire said. "The legs, the knees. What was the doctor saying?"

"I'm not sure," Evvie said. "I think maybe Sybil will have to have more surgery. He did mention an orthopedic surgeon."

"Is she going to be crippled?" Claire asked. "Sybil would hate that."

Evvie took a deep breath. "If that's what's going to happen, then we'll all have to do what we can for her," she said. "So she can adjust better."

"You mean in a wheelchair?" Thea asked. "Or on crutches?"

"I don't know," Evvie said. "Maybe. Maybe just temporarily. You know as much as I do."

Thea tried picturing Sybil in a wheelchair, but she couldn't. Sybil's face kept turning into Gina's. Thea realized that she had no idea if Gina was still alive, and Kip, in his turn, didn't know of Sybil's accident. She almost laughed, but was afraid that, if she did, she'd start crying again, so she swallowed her emotions, and lay there, absolutely still, until some form of sleep overtook her.

None of them slept past dawn the next day, and within an hour, they were back at the hospital. Sybil was getting stronger, the nurse told them. She'd awakened once, asked for her mother, and gone back to sleep. As soon as Megs heard that, she insisted that she be allowed to see Sybil, if only for a few minutes.

Clark didn't seem perturbed by last night's rejection,

but continued to stay with them in the hospital, purchasing Danish and coffee and insisting that they eat something, stretch, take walks, keep their strength up. They were in a different waiting room now, but it looked much the same as the last one, just different innocuous prints on the wall, different magazines to thumb through.

"Thea? Thea Sebastian?"

Thea turned around, expecting to see Kip. Instead she saw Peter Grass. It took her a moment to remember who he was.

"Mr. Grass," she said. "What are you doing here?"

"I read about your sister in today's paper," he said. "Are these your parents?"

Thea nodded. "And my other sisters," she said. "And friends."

Mr. Grass walked over to Nicky and Megs. "I wrote about Sybil," he said. "About the wonderful work she was doing for the poor."

"I remember," Meg said, and she was smiling and gracious and Megs-like again. "We were very proud."

"No, for tomorrow's paper," Mr. Grass declared. "I did another column about her, about how Sybil got hurt because she was trying to help others."

Thea just barely kept from yelping. She could see Claire swallow a giggle.

"That was very nice of you," Meg said. "I'm sure Sybil will enjoy reading it when she's up and about."

"She's a wonderful girl," Mr. Grass said. "How is she doing?"

"We won't know for sure for a while yet," Nick said. "But we're hopeful."

"I spoke to my editor before coming over," Mr. Grass said. "A lot of people made the connection between the news story and my original column. They remembered Sybil's name, and of course when my column appears tomorrow, even more people will remember just who Sybil is."

"That's very nice," Meg said. "I'm sure Sybil will like getting cards if people send them."

"It's more than cards," Mr. Grass said. "Two different civic groups have already called the paper about fundraisers. There's bound to be more of that sort of thing tomorrow, and all of next week. We understand that there's been extensive damage to her legs. If, I mean when, Sybil pulls through, she'll be facing a lot of physical rehabilitation."

"Fund-raisers?" Nick asked.

Peter Grass nodded. "I can give you the information if you want," he said. "I know you people are fairly new to Briarton, but this is a community that cares. And when the people feel they know someone, the way they got to know Sybil from my column, they want to reach out and help in any way they can. There's going to be an editorial tomorrow about her, as well as a call for the hit-and-run driver to turn himself in."

"That really isn't necessary," Nick said.

"We want to help," Mr. Grass said. "The whole community wants to help."

"We can take care of it ourselves," Nick said. "My family has always managed to handle its problems, and this one is no different. There will be no fund-raisers, no charity. Whatever has to be done, we'll do ourselves."

"We are grateful," Meg said, and again, that restraining hand went on Nicky's arm. "Our time in Briarton has been wonderful, and everyone at the hospital has been very kind. But we'll manage."

"They can donate blood," Sam said. "Sybil's lost a lot of blood. There's a blood shortage, anyway. My grandfather worries about that. He's a doctor. People can donate blood."

"That's fine," Mr. Grass declared. "And I'll certainly mention that to my editor. But the people of Briarton want to do more. When people open their hearts you can't just turn them away."

"Watch me," Nick said. "Now, if you'll excuse us, Mr. Grass, it's time for us to visit our daughter." He left the waiting room, and Megs trailed behind him.

"They'll change their minds," Clark said. "When the reality of the bills sets in."

"It could be too late by then," Mr. Grass replied. "Do they have any idea what they're sacrificing, what kind of money they're going to need?"

"We'll manage," Claire said, and for a moment, she was Nicky, her face, her gestures, her inflections. "We're the Sebastians, and we can take care of ourselves."

Thea stared at Claire and didn't know whether to applaud or laugh. Instead of choosing, she put her head between her knees and began to worry about money and pain and desperate desolute futures.

CHAPTER THIRTEEN

"**A**ll right," Nick said. "Here's the situation."

Thea sat in the living room. The house seemed empty, although Evvie, Claire, and Megs were there as well. Clark and Scotty had left Sunday night, and Sam had gone that morning. Evvie would be going the next day, and Thea dreaded to think how quiet things would be then.

"We know Sybil's better," Evvie declared. "They wouldn't have let me see her today if she wasn't."

Nicky nodded. "She's going to live," he said. "We're over that hurdle."

"How many more hurdles are there?" Claire asked.

"We spoke to an orthopedic surgeon this afternoon,"

Meg said. "He said it was possible Sybil might never walk again."

"That's obviously untrue," Nick said. "Sybil will walk. We'll see to that. But she's going to have to have several operations and a great deal of physical therapy."

"I don't believe it," Thea said. "If she'd been standing one foot away, or if we'd gone there twenty minutes later, none of this would have happened. I hope they find the guy who hit her and kill him."

"It was an accident," Nick said. "Maybe they'll find him, maybe they won't, but either way, Sybil's in for a long, hard spell, and we have to do everything we can to help out."

"What can I do?" Evvie asked. "I'm still willing to leave Harvard."

Megs shook her head. "Nicky and I have been talking a lot about the money," she declared. "Clark was right when he said how much was involved. But we feel very strongly that if you make it through this year, Harvard will help with the rest of your tuition. We'll have to borrow more, of course, but the one sacrifice we don't want to make is your education. Not just yours, Evvie, but Thea's and Claire's as well."

"So go back tomorrow, and work on your grades," Nick said. "The better your average, the more likely you are to wrangle some scholarship aid."

"I'll try for A's," Evvie said. "And get a part-time job."

"I can get a job, too," Thea said. "The fast-food places are always looking for kids."

"Thank you," Meg said. "Every penny is going to help."

"There's nothing I can do, right?" Claire asked. "I already go to a public school, and I'm too young to work."

"You could baby-sit," Thea said.

"Would you trust your babies with me?" Claire replied.

"Listen to me," Nick said. "We're either all in this together, or else we're no longer a family. Those are the choices. Daisy isn't going to be able to get a job, because we're going to need someone full time with Sybil, both while she's at the hospital and after she gets out. Any extra money any of us can bring in is going to go to the family. There aren't going to be any new clothes for a while, or new playthings."

"Or new pianos," Evvie said. "Oh, Megs, I'm sorry."

Megs smiled. "I can live without a piano," she said. "I still have my four daughters."

"We're going to sell the house," Nick declared.

"No!" Thea said.

"Dammit, Nicky," Claire said. "Not another dump."

"I want to finish the renovation," Meg said. "We'll get a lot higher price for it that way."

"I don't believe this," Claire said. "As soon as we get this place nice-looking, we're going to have to leave it."

"I'm also going to sell out my interest in the factory conversion," Nick said. "I have a meeting tomorrow afternoon. I'll try for the best possible price, but since the project is still in the speculative stages, we shouldn't count on my getting very much. The house is the best investment we've made, and when we sell it, we'll find a low-cost apartment to rent, and we can use the money for Sybil's care."

"Don't get me wrong," Claire said. "I love Sybil, too. But this stinks."

"Yes, it does," Nick said. "No argument."

Thea looked around the living room. Maybe in the past they'd had more money, but this was the best home she could remember them ever having. And Claire was right. "Low-cost apartment" was just a euphemism for dump. Thea knew what dumps were like, and she wasn't thrilled they'd be going back to one.

"Why not let other people help?" she asked. "Let the civic organizations have their fund-raisers. I can understand why you don't want to take money from Clark, but if the people in Briarton want to help, why turn them down?"

"There are always strings when people give you things," Nick replied. "I won't have us indebted to strangers."

"Or friends," Claire said.

"In the short run, it'll be harder," Nick said. "In the long run, you'll be grateful."

"Besides," Meg said. "We've had setbacks before. Just because Nicky's giving up on this one deal doesn't mean there won't be others. And wherever we live, it'll be our home."

"An apartment will be better for Sybil," Evvie said. "She couldn't manage the stairs here."

"How long?" Thea asked. "The operations and therapy?"

Nicky took a deep breath. "A couple of years," he replied. "Maybe more."

"We'll all help with the therapy," Meg said. "They'll train us so we'll know what to do."

"She's going to be in a lot of pain," Nick said. "And most people might quit. But not Sybil. She's a fighter, and she's going to walk again."

Thea wondered just what odds the doctor had quoted,

but then she decided it didn't matter. Nicky was right. Sybil was going to walk. She had to. They couldn't be giving up everything just to see her in a wheelchair for the rest of her life.

"I can work full-time in the summer," Evvie said. "Move back here, so in the evenings I can help out with Sybil."

"But then when would you see Sam?" Thea asked.

Evvie smiled. "I think that's the kind of sacrifice Nicky meant," she said. "Besides, if I can stay at Harvard, I'll be with him there."

"I'm glad I'm only fourteen," Claire said. "By the time I'm old enough to have to do some sacrificing, Sybil will be healthy again."

"Don't count on it," Thea muttered.

"Sybil's first operation is scheduled for Thursday," Nick said. "Barring complications."

The telephone rang. Thea was delighted to have an excuse to get away from talk of surgery and raced to the phone.

"Thea Sebastian, please."

"This is Thea," she said. "Kip?"

"Yeah," he said. "Good. I didn't know what to say if someone else answered."

"Kip, Sybil was in an accident," Thea said. "She's in the hospital."

"I know," he said. "One of the nurses told us on Saturday. I figured your family had enough going on without me, so I stayed away."

"I'm glad you called, though," Thea said. "I've missed you. I've thought about you a lot."

"Listen, Thea, Gina died," Kip said rapidly. "That's why I'm calling. Yesterday afternoon."

"Oh, God, no," Thea said.

"It was okay, it was kind of peaceful at the end," Kip said. "Mom was there, too. Gina fell asleep, and then, well, you could tell she'd died, but it was okay, it wasn't noisy or anything."

"Oh, Kip," Thea said. "How are you doing?"

"You know me, I'm fine," he replied. "Look, the funeral is tomorrow at one, and I wouldn't even bother to tell you, but Mom's been going on about it. How you were Gina's friend and all. I keep trying to explain that you really weren't, you were just a Friendly Visitor, and you have problems of your own right now, but I'm pretty sure the only way I can keep Mom sober for the funeral is if you're there. She won't show up drunk in front of you. You impress her too much. She thinks you're a lady."

"Of course I'll come," Thea said. "One o'clock. Where?"

"Chapman's Funeral Parlor on Fourth Street," Kip said. "Thanks, Thea. It'll mean a lot to Mom."

"Chapman's," Thea said. "Is there anything else I can do?"

"No," Kip said. "I'm sorry to pull you away from your own problems."

"It's all right," Thea replied. "You know how much I care about Gina."

"Right," Kip said. "Well, I'd better get off now. I'll see you tomorrow."

Thea heard him hang up. She put the phone down and walked back to the living room. "That was Kip," she said. "Gina died yesterday. Her funeral is tomorrow at one, and I told him I'd be going."

"You can't," Nick said.

"What are you talking about?" Thea asked. "Of course I can. I've missed school today, I can miss it tomorrow also."

"That's not what I'm talking about," Nick said. "My meeting is at one-thirty, and Daisy's going to have to drive Evvie to the airport for a one-forty-five flight. We need you to visit Sybil tomorrow at one."

"Why can't Claire go?" Thea asked.

"Because they won't let her in unescorted," Nick said. "If you're under sixteen, you have to come in with an adult."

"Great," Claire said. "It's an R-rated hospital."

"This is not a joking matter," Nick said. "Sybil is in constant pain, and terrified about what's ahead for her. We can't let her have any time alone to brood about Thursday's operation and the possibility of never walking again. Thea simply must be there tomorrow."

"But, Nicky," Evvie said.

"No," Nick said. "Thea understands. Her first loyalty has to be to her family."

"Oh, come on, now," Evvie said. "I can get to the airport some other way."

"Evvie, stop it," Thea said. "Nicky, my first loyalty is to the family. But it's not my only loyalty. Gina died, and Kip needs me at the funeral, and that's where I'm going to be. I'll get to Sybil's room as soon as it's over."

"Thea, I'm ordering you to visit Sybil tomorrow at the time I say," Nick said. "Call Kip back and explain to him you cannot go."

"No, Nicky," Thea said.

"That was an order," Nick said.

"I heard it," Thea replied. "And I'm ignoring it. I'm

sorry, Nicky. All my life I've gone along with what you've said, and I haven't questioned and I haven't fought. That's why I became a Friendly Visitor. Because of you. I'm still going along. You don't want us to take outside help, fine. We'll sell the house, we'll move into some lousy apartment, I'll get a job at Burger Bliss. You want me to wear rags, I'll wear rags. But tomorrow at one, I'm going to be at Gina's funeral, and there's nothing you can say that will stop me. Nothing. I'll go to the hospital as soon as I can, and I'll stay with Sybil for as long as they let me, but you have a meeting, and Megs has to drive Evvie, and I have Gina's funeral. That's just the way it is." She stared at Nicky and defied him to say another word.

Nicky stared right back. Thea waited for him to attack, but instead he nodded almost imperceptibly. "Don't linger," he said. "If they invite you to their home for cake and coffee say no."

"I would anyway," Thea said. She couldn't believe it. She had actually won a battle against Nicky. She was right and he was wrong, and they both fought fair, and she'd won. Maybe Nicky was realizing the sacrifices he was going to have to make as well.

The next day, as Thea sat in a folding chair in Chapman's Funeral Parlor's smallest chapel, she wondered if the battle had been worth it. There were seven people there, Kip, his mother and Dani, Thea, and two nurses and a doctor Thea recognized from the hospital. She remembered how Scotty had been bused to a funeral, and wished someone had imported Gina's school friends, just to cut down on the aching emptiness of the room.

Scotty was right about how boring funerals were, though.

The minister spoke briefly about Gina and her courage in facing death at such a young age, but it didn't take Thea long to realize that he'd never met Gina. One of the nurses got up then, and she did know Gina, and her words were tender and loving. Mrs. Dozier cried. Dani looked bored. Kip didn't seem to be listening.

Then the minister got up again, and spoke about heaven and eternal peace and how Gina was there with the angels. In spite of herself, Thea smiled. She hoped all the angels Gina met were as handsome as the actors in *TV Dreamstars*.

Gina's casket was open, and Thea glanced at it from time to time. Somehow the sight of Gina all made up and in a pink party dress that Mrs. Dozier probably bought for the occasion was less painful than looking at Kip or his mother or even Dani, who had managed to make her sister's funeral yet another occasion for looking cheap.

As the minister led them in the Lord's Prayer, Thea decided she hated funerals and would never go to another one again. She included her own. When the time comes, I'll swim into the ocean, she decided, and fail to swim back. She was relieved when she realized the service had ended. The doctor murmured a few words to Mrs. Dozier and left. The nurses continued to stand by her side. Dani was staring into the coffin, and Kip walked out of the room.

Thea followed him. She found him standing outside the funeral parlor. He wasn't crying, and she was glad. This is a fine occasion to repress all emotions, she thought.

"What happens next?" she asked.

"She'll be cremated," he said. "It was the cheapest way to go."

"What are you going to do with the ashes?" Thea asked. She couldn't believe she was having this conversation. Not about Gina, who had once been alive.

"I don't know," Kip said. "I've got to get out of here."

"You mean out of the funeral parlor?" Thea asked. It seemed to her he was out.

"Out of town," he said. "Today. As soon as I can."

"Why?" Thea asked. "What's your hurry?"

"I've thought about it a lot," Kip replied. "Since she died, I've hardly thought about anything else. Mom's going to leave here and get drunk, and Dani will go out cruising. If I stay tonight, I'll have to deal with them tomorrow, and then I'll be stuck here and I'll never escape. My bags are already packed. I have enough money for a bus ticket to New York and a couple of nights at a Y. I'll get a job as soon as I get there, and then I'll wait until next semester begins. I shouldn't even be standing here talking with you. I should be home right now getting my bags before Mom starts saying she can't survive without me, and Dani starts laughing and acting like a stupid, jerky kid I want to save. I mean, shake."

"You mean save," Thea declared.

"I can't," Kip said. "I can't save anyone."

"So you're just going to run away," Thea said. "Grab your bags and split, the same as your father."

"It worked for him," Kip said.

"What about me?" Thea asked. "Are you running away from me, too?"

"Thea, don't," he said.

"I have to," she said. "We've been through so much together. You can't deny our feelings."

"We haven't been through anything," Kip said. "All we've done is watch Gina die. We've never been on a date together, or laughed, or watched the sun rise. Nine times out of ten, we've met in a hospital room, and most of our conversations had to do with Gina. You expect me to have feelings for you? The only feelings I had were for Gina. Nobody else. Right now all my feelings are ashes."

"That's not true," Thea said. "I know you care for me. You can go, there's nothing I can do to stop you. But you have to admit the truth. You have to admit you love me."

Kip shook his head. "I don't love anyone," he said. "When I was a kid, I loved my mother, and the past few years I've loved Gina. Gina's gone now, and in a lot of ways Mom is, too. Fine. That's how it is. It's no big deal. But I don't love you, and that's the truth. I'm sorry, Thea. I'd like to give you your fairy tale ending. I'd like to tell you I'm free now, and we can be together. I'd like to make love to you and share rainbows and secrets and all the other romance-book dreams you seem to have. Maybe if things had been different, I would have. Maybe not. Maybe I am like my father. I don't know. I haven't had the chance to find out. And I'm not going to find out with you."

"Kip, you can't do this to me," Thea said. "Gina's death hurts me, too. And Sybil . . ."

"Dammit, don't you think I know that!" Kip shouted. "God, Thea, I've been sucked into taking care of everybody else for years and I can't do it anymore. Not for you. Not for my mother or Dani or anyone. I'm gone, Thea. You think you're talking to me, but you're not. I'm out of here already."

"No, Kip," Thea cried. She put her hand on his arm, and tried to keep him by her side.

"Oh, Thea," he said, and he started to cry. "Not now. I can't. I just can't."

Thea willed herself not to cry also. "I'll want to know where you are," she said. "When you're settled in New York, write to me."

Kip nodded. He continued to cry. Thea yearned to hold him in her arms, comfort him, make up to him for all he'd had to endure, but she knew better. She knew he was right, that what she wanted was a fairy tale ending, and it wasn't fair to ask him to come up with one.

"Are you going to be okay?" she asked. "I'll stay if you need me."

"I'm okay," he said, and he tried to smile for Thea as he had for Gina. "I need to be alone. I need to be gone."

"I know," Thea said. She put her hands on his cheeks and wiped the tears away. "You take care. And you become a wonderful sculptor. I want to see your work in museums."

Kip nodded. "I'll stay in touch," he said. "I need that, too."

"I love you," Thea said. "Just remember, that's nothing to be scared of." She stood on tiptoe, kissed him once, gently, on the lips, and walked away while she still had the strength to.

It was a twenty-minute walk to the hospital, and Thea used those twenty minutes to compose herself. She hadn't seen Sybil since the accident, and she knew it would be hard, especially since they were going to be alone. Maybe Sybil would be asleep, but if she wasn't, Thea couldn't burst into tears at the sight of her, no matter how desperately she might want to.

"She's going to walk again," she repeated over and over as she walked. "Sybil's going to be fine. We'll get through this together as a family." Families endured. Even the Doziers had in a way. And if they could, the Sebastians certainly could manage.

"I'm here to see Sybil Sebastian," she told the nurse at the desk in Sybil's ward. "Is she awake?"

"She has a visitor," the nurse replied. "Please be quiet."

"I will be," Thea said. She couldn't figure out who the visitor might be, unless Nicky had shifted his meeting so that Sybil wouldn't be alone.

But instead of Nicky, Thea found Claire sitting by Sybil's side. Claire had makeup on, and one of Megs's dresses, and high-heeled shoes. She looked at least twenty-one and more beautiful than Thea had ever seen her.

"I snuck in," she said cheerfully. "I figured I'd keep Sybil company until you got here."

"Thank you," Thea said. She couldn't remember ever having thanked Claire before for anything, except passing the salt. "Hi, Sybil. How are you?"

"I hurt all over," Sybil said, and she sounded almost like Sybil, although her mouth was swollen and her nose was bandaged. Both legs were in casts, and she had several tubes attached in the crook of her elbows. But she was still definitely Sybil. "I hurt, and I hate hospitals, and I want to go home."

"I know," Thea said, and she bent down to kiss her youngest sister. "We want you there, too. And you'll get home soon enough. Won't she, Claire?"

"I guarantee it," Claire replied. "You have to, Sybil. We're the Sebastians. We come as a matched set."

Thea swallowed down all the tears she knew she'd be shedding that evening. Tears for Gina, and Kip, and Sybil, and all the others who hurt and needed. Tears for herself, too, for the Thea who used to be, and the Thea she was becoming. There'd be time enough that evening to cry. Now, she had to be grateful that she was alive, and so was Sybil, and they were both Sebastians, and the Sebastians could get through anything as long as they stuck together.

"You're beautiful," she said. "And I love you both, and I swear, no matter how hard it is now, things are going to get better."

"Sure," Sybil said. "Wanna tell me about the tooth fairy next?"

And Thea stood by her sisters and laughed.

Follow the Sebastian sisters' trials, tribulations and triumphs in *Evvie at Sixteen*, the first title in the Sebastian Sisters series, and continuing with *Clare at Sixteen* and *Sybil at Sixteen*, the third and fourth books in the series.

ABOUT THE AUTHOR

SUSAN BETH PFEFFER graduated from New York University with a degree in television, motion pictures, and radio studies. She is a native New Yorker who now lives in Middletown, New York. Susan Beth Pfeffer is the author of many highly acclaimed young adult novels, including *The Year Without Michael*, an ALA Best Book for Young Adults and a *Publishers Weekly* Best Book of the Year, as well as *About David, Fantasy Summer,* and *Getting Even.*